MISSION IMPOSSIBLE

Beth Goobie

NORTHERN LIGHTS YOUNG NOVELS

Red Deer College Press

Copyright © 1994 Beth Goobie

NORTHERN LIGHTS YOUNG NOVELS ARE PUBLISHED BY
Red Deer College Press
56 Avenue & 32 Street Box 5005
Red Deer Alberta Canada T4N 5H5

5 4 3 2

ACKNOWLEDGMENTS
Edited for the Press by Tim Wynne-Jones
Cover art by Jeffery Hitch
Design by Dennis Johnson
Printed and bound in Canada
for Red Deer College Press

Financial support provided by the Alberta Foundation for the Arts, a beneficiary of the Lottery Fund of the Government of Alberta, and by the Canada Council, the Department of Communications and Red Deer College.

COMMITTED TO THE DEVELOPMENT OF CULTURE AND THE ARTS

CANADIAN CATALOGUING IN PUBLICATION DATA
Goobie, Beth, 1959–
Mission impossible
(Northern lights young novels)
ISBN 0-88995-114-4
I. Title. II. Series.
PS8563.O8326M5 1994 jC813'.54 C94-910150-8
PZ7.G66Mi 1994

Contents

For Alberta Cole and for Peter:
Thank you for my voice

WATERFALL

The point up for debate is whether or not life is a worth-while proposition—a serious proposition. Perhaps, as a point of clarification, is life an advisable career option?

I mean, thought Jill as she studied the pink poster, if you're really going to take life seriously, to the point of investing in long-term RRSPs . . . Like, if you're planning, someday, to evolve into a senior citizen, you need to learn what it's all about, this Life Stuff, the penalties and benefits of being alive. And how you make the benefits outweigh the penalties.

THE LOVELY LEGS COMPETITION . . .

Jill regarded the poster morosely. It was stapled to a maple just outside the high school's front entrance, and Jill's eyes had zeroed in on the pink. She hated pink.

The mid-September sky sulked just above her mood. Jill glared at the clouds. "For once, the cosmos and I are in sync," she muttered. "Could they have picked a better day?" Jill stuck her hands into the pockets of her black sweats, found a penny and began to play with it. She continued to study the poster.

SPONSORED BY THE WARRIORS . . .

Of course, the football team was involved, probably led by her brother, Captain Dwayne Gilbert. She read on.

AND THE TELEGRAPH.

Her newspaper—leader of free thought and challenger of the status quo. Anger shifted in her stomach. Jill pressed her fingers against the penny's edges. Funny how emotions never seemed to affect the external world. The grass still wore its green grin. The school's red brick was as oblivious as usual.

Assumptions—that's what it was all about. Jill worked the penny in her pocket, flipping its faces. Assumptions that everybody would think this competition would be fun, good for school spirit and social order and that the few who did disagree were nobodies anyway. Too many people were around these days, thought Jill. If you wanted to count, you had to be a hundred votes, not one. The other option was to become the captain of the football team. In her brother's case, that meant you had to act as if you were followed at all times by twenty invisible cheerleaders, waving pompoms as if their self-esteem depended upon it.

The school doors opened, and bodies rushed out toward her, their sound and size looming larger as they approached. No one stopped to look at the poster or Jill. They moved past as if she did not exist. Jill waited. It had been automatic—as they approached, she had stiffened, resisting. Resisting what? Jill wondered, pulling the coin out of her pocket. The penny had imprinted red welts into her thumb and fingertips. She shrugged and hitched her black knapsack higher up her right shoulder. She would work up a dinner-table speech for big brother Dwayne. He could not chew potatoes and meat louder than she could talk. She would hide dessert until he agreed to listen.

Two weeks ago, she had heard him out, through his entire verbal rampage about her trying out for the football team.

"What d' you plan to do with your boobs when you get tackled?" he had demanded.

"And what d' you do with your brains when a thought hits?" she had asked.

There had been no answer. Dwayne considered silence his ultimate point in a debate.

JILL HAD DEVELOPED a theory about the intricacies of peer interactions. Summed up, it was: You never can tell, but don't hold your breath.

On the surface, the different social groups looked about as firmly established as layers of rock in the Canadian Shield. But every now and then, strata shifted an inch—a piece of shale broke off, a pebble went on a roll.

Summer was like that, giving small shoves this way and that, bleaching, tanning, toning. The chain smoker endured a two-month nic fit at Grandpa's and Grandma's, came back breathing more easily and joined the soccer team. The nerd got contacts and took up long-distance cycling. A drug dealer moved to the youth detention center, and a track and field star took over her clientele. Pregnant, a girl might drop out.

All this meant that the first couple of weeks in the school year were about discovering or reinforcing your personal stratum. Not that there were a lot of options. The Canadian Shield hadn't changed much in eons and neither had the basic social groups. Jill figured most of it was pretty much decided at birth.

The smoking crowd was the founding layer. It was also the first clique to set up regular meetings along sidewalks or huddled in school entrances. Some of the kids wore ACDC or Def Leppard tee shirts and sported crude tattoos, imprinted with pins and ball-point pens. Jill always felt uneasy walking through their brooding groups, wondering how many of them were coming down or going up and whether she was in their way.

Then there were the shop kids, some of whom were not in the smoking crowd. Next were the nerds. They were usually quite thin or thick, paler than three-ring binder paper, out of date, out of style, out of mind. Above them settled the stratum whose overwhelming mediocrity banned them from any other definitive group. C+ and B students, they played third clarinet for four years running in the school band or sat on the bench, never quite good enough to make the field. Talent formed the second-to-top layer, as long as it was not purely intellectual. This was the respect given to the successful class clown, student council member, the drama crowd. And of course, on the top were the athletes, swaggering in their assumptions of good health and beautiful bodies.

Jill did not like the options. It was too cold too much of the year to stand out in the middle of ice, snow and an unsympathetic wind, the only source of heat being a three-inch cigarette. To thoroughly establish yourself, it seemed necessary to rush out during school breaks in shirt sleeves and goose bumps, with holes in jean knees and upper inside thighs providing additional contact with the north wind.

As for the shop crowd, Jill was barely able to distinguish a hammer from a bulldozer. Her brain waves were far too unpredictable to be a nerd. So were her report cards. She had joined the chess club, which, she supposed, placed her in the company of breathtaking intellectual standards. But she despised the eagerness of the Reach For The Top team, their unmitigated glee at being able to arrange the proper words in the proper order to answer, "Who invented the filing cabinet?" or "What are bowling pins made of?" Jill figured she had better things to do with her mind.

Perhaps she was mediocre. But she knew her behavior quirks had provoked occasional moments of stardom. She had demolished the school principal's car with a driver training vehicle. And she had tried out for the football team. But if she identified herself with the talent crowd, it would be a self-proclaimed compliment, suspicious in nature.

All Jill did know was that she refused, on principle, to be an athlete. She had condemned herself to wandering between the social groups, sidestepping any expectations she saw headed her way.

WHEN DWAYNE WALKED IN, he demanded the whole room. Maybe it was his aura, Jill thought. Maybe his aura lifted weights just like he did. Whatever the reason, she had always felt her brother's charisma overpower her. Even her own body space seemed to become less her own when he was near. If she was temporarily required to support one of his opinions, she felt his gaze clamp her so tightly she could hardly breathe. Then his eyes would flick her aside like a throw cushion.

"It was your editor's idea," Dwayne pointed out. He squirted a quarter inch of mustard across a cold wiener sandwich, his preferred after-school snack.

Jill watched him eat with her usual distaste. Two years ago, she had insisted on moving to the opposite side of the dinner table to avoid being assaulted by chunks of food that missed his mouth. A discouraging realization had accompanied this change of position—Dwayne had not seemed to notice.

"He came to me as the football team captain and suggested the event as a *prelude* to the Christmas assembly." Dwayne emphasized the word *prelude*, Jill noted, to underline his knowledge of its existence.

"Advertising a little early, don't you think?"

"Anticipation." Dwayne savored the word.

"And Ewald suggested it to you?"

"Yup," Dwayne affirmed. He returned the mustard to the fridge and picked up his sandwich. She had been dismissed.

"It's sexist." Jill realized that in a conversation with Dwayne all this could produce was a rhetorical shrug.

"It's a tradition," he winked, turning to go. "It's biological. Girls have sexy legs. Why fight nature?"

His blue eyes were grinning, but not at her. What was he enjoying?

Then it came to her. Power. Some sort of power.

"Guys have sexy legs, too," her mouth snapped.

Dwayne snorted and rubbed one hand through his short light-brown hair. "Sexy to who?"

"Sexy to girls."

The power of assumption, she thought. There it is again.

"Yeah, but you don't see us walking around in nylons," said Dwayne. He took a few steps to the door.

"What's that got to do with it?" Jill cried. Her voice skyrocketed out of her control.

Dwayne turned in the doorway and leaned against the frame. He took a bite and chewed methodically. "Look, Jill." He had switched to his Advice Tone. "You can't expect the whole world to be like you. Boycott the dance. Boycott the contest. That seems to be your solution to everything else."

"Boycott the mainstream, eh?" muttered Jill.

"It's your choice," Dwayne shrugged. "Nobody's making you." Another bite out of his sandwich, a direct implacable stare and Dwayne left.

Jill heard him mount the stairs to the second floor. Even his footsteps were regular. Nothing about him was unexpected. He had set all precedents for thinking and behavior in grade three.

Her emotions, on the other hand, were zooming around like some video game. She hated that. If she could just get a grip. Then maybe she could figure out why she was so angry, why she could not seem to get along with anybody. Why she kept shoving people away.

It was just that she had never been able to reconcile herself to assumptions.

"Or pink," she muttered to the empty kitchen.

JILL DECIDED TO RESOLVE matters in the usual fashion. She adjusted her Selective Memory Dial and eliminated that little conversation with brother Dwayne in the kitchen. She also eliminated the mustard and cold wiener sandwich. Better not to pass any hint of that barbaric ritual on to posterity. She thought she would like to take the process further and eliminate Dwayne completely from her conscious reality, simply pull the plug on their relationship. But she had tried it before, and he had not gone away.

Mediocrity. That was the biggest problem, Jill fretted. Her life was boring. She decided to give herself the usual emotional promotion, flicked the stereo switch and settled onto the living-room floor. Ennio Morricone's music began.

Jill had watched the movie *The Mission* seven times so far. She had listened to the soundtrack so often, she had worn down one record and replaced it with a CD. Still, she had not been able to decide what drew her to this story, sucked her into it.

Knees to her chin, she listened.

The movie's plot was based on historical fact. It concerned the interaction of three white men with the Guaraní Indians, who lived above a giant waterfall at the borders between Argentina, Paraguay and Brazil. There was a Jesuit priest who gained the friendship of the Guaraní through music. He opposed a second man, a slave trader, who hunted the Guaraní and sold them as slaves to the Portuguese and Spanish. After the slave trader killed his own brother in a duel, he could not live with himself, so the Jesuit persuaded him to come and visit the Guaraní. The forgiveness of the Guaraní taught the slave trader the meaning of love and relationship, and he joined the Jesuit Order.

Jill decided that one of the reasons she listened to the soundtrack was because it made her bawl without having to think about it, in an abstract sort of way. She could get all the crap out of her system without having to figure out what was really bothering her. It was true that the friendship between the slave trader, the Jesuit and the Guaraní would have been enough to produce her big Bawl And Weep Scenario but there was more to it than that.

Because of the Treaty of Madrid, the territory the Guaraní inhabited passed from Spanish to Portuguese hands. The Pope sent out a papal legate, named Altamarino. Everyone in the movie called him "His Eminence." The Jesuit missionaries were all that protected the Guaraní from slave traders, and it was up to His Eminence to decide whether the Jesuits stayed or left. Actually, he was only supposed to pretend to decide. He knew before he came to the Jesuit mission that European politics required the Jesuits to leave.

With the introduction of His Eminence, the music became part of the movie's plot in a manner that boggled Jill's brain. His Eminence came out, largely as a formality, to affirm for the Europeans that the Guaraní were savages and not worth the effort of salvation. However, the Guaraní were very musical and had learned some of the traditional music of the Catholic church. They sang for His Eminence. The scenes that followed had imploded themselves into Jill's brain and would not go away.

A young boy sang a solo for His Eminence. His Eminence walked into a church full of singing Guaraní. In the middle of the street, His Eminence was surrounded by Guaraní, dancing and playing instruments. His Eminence watched the Guaraní. Sometimes his face fought his delight. Mostly, his face remained absolutely still.

How can he do this? Jill wondered. Every time she watched these scenes, she thought, His Eminence knows he's going to order the Jesuits to leave. He knows the Portuguese army will come in, then enslave or kill the Guaraní. His Eminence has to sit there and absorb the most beautiful music he's heard in his entire life, knowing he'll allow the singers to die.

And it happened. His Eminence did tell the priests to leave. Then he went down river. The priests refused to go, and the Portuguese army invaded. Some of the Guaraní fought back alongside the slave trader. Some of them prayed and sang in the church with the Jesuit. The soldiers shot them all—those who fought back and those who sang.

It was all very confusing—the movie, all those deaths, the stuff that went on in His Eminence's head. She was not sure why she kept coming back to it, why it seemed so important. But it was important. It made all the Pale Pastel Boring High School and I Hate My Brother Junk go away.

As usual, the music got inside and shifted around in her stomach. Jill started to cry. It gave her a headache. After the music was over, she washed her face with cold water. Then she went on with the average functions of another boring mediocre day.

JILL'S MOTHER SAT in the brown armchair and observed Jill over her knitting. Having a mother who spoke three different languages was dangerous. Jill could never be sure whether her mother could translate Jill's silence into words, too.

"What do you want to do about the competition, Jill?" asked her mother.

Jill sat on the floor, picking small pieces of noncarpet off the carpet. Leftovers of time, she mused.

"I dunno," she said. "I mean, what can I do? What does it really matter anyway?"

"You're angry, aren't you?"

"Yeah," said Jill slowly. "But I'm not sure why. I mean, I don't have the right to stop them. There's nothing wrong with it."

"Then why are you angry?"

"There's something I don't get about this whole thing."

"Yes?"

"Well, how come I feel like this competition is an insult to me? It doesn't make sense. Like, even if I'm not up on that stage. Even if I'm in the audience, or even if I boycott the whole thing and I don't go to watch it . . . I mean, what if I don't even leave the house that day? I don't even go to school. I stay in my room. I stay in my bed! It'll still feel like it's me up there on that stage, like it's my legs they're judging. I must be the definition of paranoia."

"No, it makes sense to me," said Jill's mother. She frowned at her knitting.

"How come?"

"Because they're judging those girls, not as individuals but as objects."

"Objects?" said Jill. "I guess. But they're choosing to go up on stage and be objects. They don't have to."

Her mother fished at a dropped stitch. Then she paused, tapping a finger against a needle. "The competition is a one-time event. But anyone who participates in it, as audience or judge or competitor, has been living out that competition all along."

"Oh," said Jill, "I guess."

Her mother interrupted enthusiastically. "And if you accept it as a competition, you accept it as a philosophy," she announced with great satisfaction. "So, boycotting the competition isn't enough of a statement for you?"

"Nobody will notice or care," Jill said flatly, pushing her small collection of lint under her mother's chair. "They'll be too busy looking at all the legs on stage."

"So maybe that's where you need to be then, dear." Jill's mother broke off her wool. "Up on stage."

"On stage?" gasped Jill. "As a competitor?!"

"Being a feminist means being uncomfortable," said her mother. "You have to work to make yourself a visible minority. You do have alternatives. And power."

"So you're telling me one of my options is to get up on stage," said Jill. She pushed her entire mouth to the right side of her face. This was very confusing. Brain Warp.

"I suppose so."

"Isn't that, like, playing along with the whole image?" Jill demanded.

"Oh, I didn't suggest you play along with their image," replied her mother calmly.

"Well, what are you saying, then?"

"Oh, I don't want to tell you what to do."

"That's not fair, Mom."

"Life's not fair," replied her mother.

THE YEAR'S SECOND MEETING of the *Telegraph* committee was in progress. Jill sat next to Ewald, editor for the past three years. Nobody else seemed to want the job. As this was Jill's second meeting, she still felt like a pin among needles, a radish among plums.

"Deadline for the first issue is next Wednesday," said Ewald. "Rob, you'll get the sports done?"

"Yup," said Rob.

"Susan, what's your book of the month?"

"It's a Stephen King, *Dolores Claiborne,*" said Susan.

"Couldn't you find any Canadian trash?" sighed Ewald.

"Nothing anyone's heard of."

"Wednesday," sighed Ewald again. "Jill, I've got the survey question for you. It has to do with future career choices. Counseling Services wants it done." He handed her a piece of paper.

"Oh," said Jill. Yuck, she thought. Already she hated the idea. She had a suspicion the size of a monsoon that the position of survey taker was the bottom rung on the *Telegraph* promotion ladder.

"Okay, any questions?" asked Ewald.

Jill cleared the cork in her throat. The words popped out. "How come the *Telegraph* is backing that legs competition?"

Ewald shrugged. "It was just a suggestion," he said. "I was going to bring it up for discussion."

"But the poster is already printed," Jill pointed out.

Where the hell had those words come from? Jill wished very much that she had not said any of them or that someone else had said all of them.

"Jill, we serve a student body," Ewald muttered.

"In nylons and a mini-skirt?"

Who the hell had control of her mouth? Shut up, shut up, shut up, Jill, she thought.

"Can I finish?" Ewald demanded. He definitely looked threatened. When nervous, Ewald had a habit of unbuttoning his shirt. This habit had catapulted him into notoriety. Everyone in every social strata of Ewald's grade waited for the mandatory English speech competitions. Ewald fell apart in front of a crowd, undressed, in fact. (Definition of a crowd? Two, three . . . on a good day, six.)

"You have no hair on your chest," Rob observed.

Ewald hastily buttoned his shirt. "Do we want to vote on it now?" he asked.

Jill looked around. The five other members of the *Telegraph* committee lay slumped over their desks in various positions of disinterest.

"Fine with me," Rob shrugged. "It'll fit right in with the sports column. I'll give it a promo." He grinned at Jill.

"We could make it an issue for the monthly survey," suggested Susan.

"Go with the flow," shrugged Renita.

"I only have an opinion on layout," chomped Beth. All of her words appeared in a pink bubble. Her vowels sounded round.

Jill's guilt picked up the megaphone in her brain. It roared at her: The majority of the student body are fairly normal. The guys play football, wear rugby shirts and read *Playboy*. The girls get perms, wear nail polish and try out for the cheerleading team. Most of them do not attempt to get on the football team, not even to make a point. Most of them have no point to make. They do not play chess. They do not listen to CBC radio. Most of these students are not you, do not like the things you do and do not adhere to your opinions.

Jill turned down the volume on her guilt. "Well, it's just that I don't see how we approved this without talking about it first. Did you check it out with the staff adviser?"

Rob hooted. "Coach?! He drooled at the thought." Rob gave Jill a sultry wink.

"Have you got something in your eye?" she growled.

"Yeah, you." Then he snorted off and on for the next five minutes, ending up with the hiccups.

"Majority rule," sighed Ewald.

Majority ignore, Jill corrected silently.

"IT WAS JUST ONE of those moments of specific insanity," said Jill.

She was facing Calvin Harding across The Chessboard. Because he was the Wellington County champion, any chessboard became The Chessboard with him on its other boundary. This was the first time she had played against him, and expecting to win would have been an unmitigated break with reality.

"The *Telegraph* has always been the voice of the middle class," said Cal. "Ewald is a coward."

"Nerves like a barbed-wire fence," muttered Jill.

"Tell you what," said Cal. "Since this is your first game against me, I'll take off both my rooks."

Two other games were in progress. "Ooooooo," commented one of the other boys. "That's quite a handout."

Cal shrugged and hunched forward. "No problem."

Mr. Fizell, the staff supervisor, sat at his desk, marking French vocab quizzes. He grinned. "You haven't played Jill yet."

Cal shrugged again. He was quite pale and had dark curly hair down to his shoulders. It made him look a little like a medieval page. When in complex thought, he grabbed onto his hair with both hands and held on. "You can have the first move," he said.

Cal was an intellectual skyscraper. He thought so fast that if you were not careful, his comments could give your brain whiplash. Jill pushed her queen's pawn forward two squares. Cal leaned forward, stroking his chin, then moved out a knight.

When Jill played chess, her brain squeezed every thought so hard that her head ached. Her eyes gouged out potential moves on the board. Though she did not know how to plan ahead, she was careful to cover every move. Her favorite pieces were rooks—straight and simple. As soon as she could, she got one out front.

The other games finished. The four boys wandered over and folded themselves into nearby desks, watching. Mr. Fizell completed his papers, came over and stood above the board. A long spindly man, he seemed to continually attach his hand to his chin.

Jill was aware that as a new member and the only female, she was not expected to make more than the minimal contribution of showing up. She had beaten Roger Acker last week in a lunch-time game, but he could not distinguish a king from a queen. She felt a dull hunger. It was a quarter to five. The room seemed to move in and out with the slow breathing of the surrounding boys. Jill wanted to go home for supper. She thought her position was okay; she was up a pawn, but Cal's brain had evolved millennia beyond his peers. He had probably given that piece to her as an early step toward her annihilation. She thought of suggesting a raincheck—possibly several generations later. She looked at the other boys.

They were all staring at the board. Mr. Fizell had his hand over his mouth, but Jill could tell he was grinning. "Take a look at your bishop, Jill," he said.

Cal was hanging by his hair. "No help!" he snapped. His eyes torpedoed the board. The other boys, too, could not yank their eyes off her game. Maybe there was something important happening on the board, she thought. Something she had missed.

"You're sunk, Harding," said one of the boys.

Suddenly, Jill's bishop felt like an old friend. What are you hiding from me? she asked it silently. You want to just kind of point your little hat in the right direction when the others aren't looking? But everyone else had fixed a dead stare on that piece. Better not, she advised the bishop silently.

Limply, Jill fingered several possibilities. Pawn, bishop and knight? No. Queen, pawn, then bishop? Yeah, sure—leave your back row exposed. Bishop and rook? Oh! Bishop and rook!

Surprise caught at her throat. She looked at Cal. He had slumped forward until he hovered, nose three inches above his king. Mr. Fizell gave a low undercover chuckle and walked back to his desk.

Jill moved her bishop. Beside her, a boy hooted, slamming his palm flat on the desktop. "You're a goner, Cal!"

Emphatically, Cal moved a piece. Sudden fear jerked Jill. Was this something she hadn't noticed? She checked, her eyes voracious. No, it did nothing. She moved her rook.

"Checkmate," she whispered.

The boys hooted. They cheered. They banged on their desks and shoved Cal on the shoulder so that he swayed in his seat. Now that it was over, Jill's mind felt like a wet paper bag. Cal's eyes mourned the board.

"Thanks for the game," she said timidly. "I wish everyone I played took off their rooks."

Cal pulled his nose off the game and gave her an embarrassed glance. "I won't do it again," he said grimly. "Good game."

Mr. Fizell shoved back his chair. "Are you free next Saturday, Jill? We need a fourth player at a tournament in Kitchener."

"Yeah, sure," said Jill. "That'd be great."

"Drop in, three or four times next week to practice up," advised Mr. Fizell. "Okay, everybody out of here. I'm hungry."

JILL HOOKED her fingers through the wire fence that surrounded the school's practice football field. Above her, maples exploded into late September orange and red against a blue sky. Kids hung about, smoking, leaning on their bikes, kicking at fallen leaves. Jill watched her brother.

He seemed like a foreign object, out there among the other guys. All of them did, in those football pads and funny tight pants. Jill did not attend the high school games and had never watched one on TV. This meant she had not progressed past her first reaction to the visual image of football players. The odd moment that she caught glimpses of the school team with their tight little bums and hulking shoulders, they seemed like some sort of surrealistic joke. She always giggled.

Dwayne was doing a quick run-stop-run pattern while the coach shouted. Sounds rude, Jill thought. Why let someone yell at you like that? She sighed. She had seen other girls, their eyes like petunias, moan about Dwayne and call him gorgeous. Once, without asking, she had borrowed his coat and found condom packages in a pocket. She had never seen a condom before.

The chain fence felt good against her small breasts, her abdomen, softened some of the hard lines that ran through her muscles. Gradually, her mind stopped spinning around inside her skull, and her thoughts slowed down.

Why couldn't they get along? she wondered. They never talked to each other unless one of them was in the bathroom and the other wanted in. Through some quirk in the high school scheduling, they had ended up in the same social history class, despite the different grades they were in. "Probably a computer virus," she had consoled him.

Dwayne had threatened to sue the school secretaries. "Just keep your mouth glued," he had warned her.

Jill shared his antipathy to any peer recognition of their shared genetic origin so she had cooperated. On school property, the two of them did not interact unless Dwayne forgot his lunch. If anyone mentioned her connection to Dwayne Gilbert, Jill produced a very blank stare and very soon into the semester, nobody did.

Way back in grade school, they had been best buds, built a tree house, fought off the next-door neighbor kids with imaginary laser guns. It had not been until grade five or six that she had noticed how Dwayne could move people around himself as easily as his own fingers. He seemed to get whatever he wanted from anyone, including her.

Two years his junior, she had transferred into junior high the year Dwayne transferred to high school. Teachers and older students kept saying she looked just like him. They expected her to do the same things, like the same things: school sports teams, student council.

And she did like these things. That was the problem. To get everyone to see that she was her own person, she had to search out the alternatives to Dwayne's reputation. That meant choosing activities her brother ignored. She joined the chess club. She had a brief unmusical fling with the bassoon. It was about this time that she made her sudden fashion revolution to an all-black wardrobe. She even began to study, and she joined the reading club. And every time Dwayne walked into a room assuming she wanted to do something he wanted to do, something she had always liked up to that year, she told him off and walked out.

She seemed to have gotten what she wanted. Without discussion, they had become official strangers, kids with similar surnames and nothing more. Everyone had forgotten her connection to Dwayne Gilbert. Including Dwayne. She was different. She was her own person. And she was lonely.

She took one last look at the field. Dwayne rammed himself against the heavy sandbags with an energy that made Jill's stomach clench. The rest of the team kept up their steady grunts and groans. She decided to go walk the train tracks up past the Edinburgh Road crossing. There was a section with trees on both sides where the tracks stretched into a long curve. Jill liked it there, where the trees muffled sounds of traffic and the rails ran on into a great silence. On the greyest days, especially in the rain, Jill would stand midpoint on the curve, balancing on a rail. There was the feeling that time had given her a piece of the afternoon off, that she had been left alone without the need to hear, see or respond. Alone this way, she could be at peace, a temporary stop between past and future.

JILL LOCKED her bedroom door. She positioned herself at one end of her bedroom, facing her floor-length mirror, which was attached to the opposite wall. Her reflection looked a little like a used twist-tie. She straightened her shoulders. The not-good-enough hair, the not-good-enough face, the decidedly substandard body—she felt as if she was facing an opponent. Kind of like chess, she mused. If I can knock that reflection out of existence, I win.

She bent her head down to her knees and fluffed her hair. That gave her a little more of the windblown look . . . in a Guelph bedroom, without a draft. Reality Warp. Not bad, she thought, but it was about time a bosom showed up.

"Okay, now." She pressed her Casual Walk Button and sauntered the length of the room. She paid severe attention to hip movement, wanting to avoid a pendulum swing. Then she returned to her former position and tried it again. Too jerky—she looked like a VW Bug with a neurotic at the clutch.

Pretend that Peter—gorgeous guy from science—is standing down the hall. Jill fluffed her hair again. She tried out her I'm A Friendly Female But Not A Slut Face and walked up to the mirror again. She stopped, looked herself in the eyes, put on a Surprised But Not Startled Expression and said, "Oh, hi!"

Her blue eyes had their glassy demeanor. With her light-brown hair and rather square face, she did look just like Dwayne. "Oh, yeah," she said. "Peachy. Try a smile with teeth."

Jill backed away from the mirror, added a few inches to the hip swing and bared her molars. Dracula/Bugs Bunny mix. "Hi there!" she cried enthusiastically. "I dine on carrot cake." She switched to a drawl. "And vast barrels of blood."

Jill decided to can her image-revitalization plan in favor of a chocolate chip cookie.

JILL WAS LISTENING to *The Mission* soundtrack. She studied the CD cover. It was a painting of a giant horseshoe waterfall. A man was on a cross, plummeting over the falls, facing down.

At the beginning of the movie, there had been another Jesuit priest. He had not lasted very long. He had also worked among the Guaraní, but something about the place had twisted his brain so that he got the natives to tie him onto a cross. Then they pushed him and the cross out from shore so he traveled down the river and over the giant falls.

Jill thought this was pretty stupid. Why the heck would anyone shove off down a river to get his head bashed in on some anonymous rock? Or drown on the way down?

But the painting of the water was beautiful. It rushed over the CD cover in pinks, blues, browns and white. It made her think of the music, the way it seemed to move and weave through itself.

She wondered about that moment at the edge of the waterfall, when the man began to slide down and saw his death coming at him. Would he feel glory or horror? He must have decided, Jill thought, that as they tied him to the cross, it would be glory. Would he have had the time or inclination to change his mind with the rushing of all that water in his ears?

DEB HAD EATEN most of the sour cream and onion chips. She was developing a hefty line of plaque around her braces. She poked at her glasses with a greasy knuckle and sighed.

"I think that periods really are the curse. I had to stay in bed a whole day this week. I couldn't even go to school. Extra Strength Tylenol didn't do a thing."

"Is that why you missed Latin?" Jill asked.

It was Friday night. Her parents had gone to a performance at the Guelph Little Theater. Dwayne was at a party. Deb had come over to watch *The Breakfast Club* on the VCR with Jill. They were munching away, consolidating energy for it. After this, there was the bag of Cheesies.

"Yeah."

"Didn't miss much."

"I dunno," said Deb. "I think someone should figure out some way of giving guys periods, don't you think?"

"Then they'd always be coming into the girls washrooms to get at the tampons," Jill observed.

Deb shrieked. "I don't really mean every month. I just think it would be good if they knew what it felt like, y' know? All the mess. It's so gross."

"I heard guys are on a fifteen-minute cycle," said Jill.

"Fifteen-minute cycles!" cried Deb.

"Yeah. Erection, ejaculation, erection, ejaculation," said Jill. "Every fifteen minutes. I read it somewhere."

"No!" said Deb. "Really?"

"Yup," said Jill. She got this way around Deb. Boredom sharpened her wit, made her feel as if she ran a solo *Saturday Night Live*.

"Let's start the Cheesies," she said. "You seen this movie before?"

"Three times," said Deb. "I cry my eyes out every time."

Jill wondered what Dwayne was doing at his party. She

wondered why she hung around with Deb. She turned on the movie and tried to forget about things.

TIRED AFTER A LATE NIGHT, Jill spent the ride to the Kitchener tournament watching the countryside go by. Most of the conversation was chewed out between Cal and Mr. Fizell. The boy aimed his opinions like a Frisbee. Never disagree with this guy, Jill told herself silently.

The tournament was set up in a high school cafeteria. Mr. Fizell went directly to the registration table. The boys headed off toward the food counter. Jill stood close to the cafeteria entrance and observed. She was the only girl. The realization tasted similar to turnip. So, if there was one other girl, Jill scolded, would I run over and strike up an immediate lifelong bonding process with her? Get real—guys are people. With penises.

They were, after all, mostly nerds—the thin sort, with glasses hitchhiking on their faces. But a few looked as if they might harbor some mainstream interests. Jill practiced long slow breathing against the pitter patter of tiny nerves in her stomach. I am scared, she told herself. In fact, I feel slightly hysterical.

Mr. Fizell returned. "I've got the schedule for the first round," he announced.

"Am I the only girl?" Jill asked.

"Yup," grinned Mr. Fizell. "But don't think we'll go easy on you because of that." He tossed her a consoling comment. "Just do your best, Jill. That's all we expect on the first try."

Jill lost her first match. Then she lost her second. Cal won them both easily. The other two boys pulled a win and draw between their four games. On the third round, irritated by her opponent's prophetic grin, Jill lost again in less than ten minutes.

A photographer stopped by their board. "I'm from the *Kitchener-Waterloo Record,*" he said. "Mind if I take a picture for the paper?"

"Of me?" Jill asked.

"We don't usually get girls at these events. Good publicity."

"As long as you don't publish my score," Jill said.

"Sure," the man grinned.

Cal placed first. All the way back to Guelph, Jill pondered. Twenty-seven competitors, I'm the only girl and I come in last. Twenty-seven competitors, I'm the only girl and I come in last. Twenty-seven competitors, I'm the only girl . . .

" . . . AND ON SATURDAY, our chess team, with its latest star member, Jill Gilbert, traveled to Kitchener. They managed to pull a fourth in the tournament. Congratulations. That's it for sports."

Her name on the PA. Everyone in the school had heard her name on the PA. Rob. He made that announcement. This is a problem, Jill thought. She had just wanted to play on the chess team, not have her reputation destroyed. She had not wanted every functioning brain unit in the entire high school to acquire the knowledge that she was a member of the chess team.

"Dork," she muttered, pushing her pen around on her desk.

The girl who sat ahead of Jill in homeroom swiveled around in her seat. "Congratulations, Jill. I didn't know you played chess."

"Thanks," Jill muttered.

"DOESN'T THE CHESS TEAM usually come in first?" Dwayne's vowels smelled like meatloaf. "Must've lost more games than usual."

"Must you be so direct?" asked Jill.

"Well, Cal would've won all his games," Dwayne said. "How'd you get on the team, anyway?"

Jill glared, needlessly. Dwayne had already refocused on his potatoes. "They checked with the football team," she said, "but of course nobody there has graduated beyond checkers. So they were stuck with me."

"What a lovely dinner you made, dear," interrupted their mother in pointed tones.

"Why, thank-you," said their father, in his This Is Family Time Voice. "How's the survey coming along, Jill?"

"I haven't started yet," Jill muttered. "It's a lousy question."

Dwayne snorted. "Nobody wants that job. It's just a way for the office to haul in information. Everybody got so tired of last year's survey taker, they tied him up and gagged him."

"Next time, I'm going to make up my own question," said Jill. She was doing her best to appear as if that last morsel of pertinent information was not as pertinent as it sounded. Dwayne looked at her for the first time. A laugh outlined his entire face.

"You are being rude," commented their father, switching to his Quit Picking On Jill Voice. "You're on dishes tonight, remember?"

"Yeah, I remember." Dwayne continued to eat silently, keeping the grin.

Jill picked up the catsup and wrote *jerk* across her meatloaf. Then she swiveled her plate. Dwayne had enough problems reading right side up.

JILL POURED the upper half of her body across the cafeteria table. Egg salad sandwiches were Ultimate Boredom. Why had she made egg salad sandwiches? She opened one eye and fixed it on Deb, who was very involved with her french fries and gravy.

"Deb, what d' you want to be when you grow up?"

"A nurse," said Deb, swallowing. "I read a coupla good books about nursing. I think that'd be a nice thing to be, don't you think?" She picked up a fry and studied its angles, a speck of grease on her lower lip.

"Sure," said Jill. Lethargically, she slid her clipboard over and wrote down *Nurse*. She already had three other *Nurses*.

"How come you're writing it down?"

"It's for the *Telegraph* survey."

27

"You're putting my answer in the *Telegraph?*" demanded Deb. She set down the fry.

"Yeah. Does this mean you want to change it?" asked Jill.

"Well, I dunno. I'll have to think about this." Faced with a decision, Deb seemed to have lost her appetite.

"Has to be in on Wednesday," said Jill. Should she brave the egg salad? Major Emotional Risk.

"Hmmm," pondered Deb. "I dunno. A secretary? What about a secretary? I'm taking typing."

Maybe buy an ice cream sandwich, Jill thought. Major Calorie Risk. Live a little.

JILL'S SCIENCE PARTNER, Arlene, was an athlete. She had been late the day the seating plan was drawn up, and the only remaining seat had yawned next to Jill. Arlene had stood by the empty seat and stared at her accusingly. Sharing a term at a desk with Jill meant a possible plunge in Arlene's social standing, and Jill had felt responsible, as if she had been plotting Arlene's downfall. Briefly, she had wished for any sort of transformation: into a Bunsen burner, a shoelace, the nearby wall chart on mitosis. She said nothing as Arlene reluctantly deposited her very popular butt on the stool. From that point on, Jill attempted to improve the situation by being as nonpresent as possible.

Arlene put up with her. For the most part, conversation was nonexistent. Boys with broad shoulders and deep voices lounged on Arlene's half of the desk until class started. During these time capsules, Jill feigned a desperate interest in conjugating Latin verbs.

Her pretended oblivion was a classic failure. The boys' shoulders crowded her thoughts, rubbed against her mind. She hated this. Driving the pen tip hard against the binder paper did not help. The sounds of the boys' voices made her grow hot, caused her IQ to fade in and out. And with the deterioration of her IQ, Jill knew her mouth kicked in to compensate, increasing the potential for verbal disasters. She sweated it out until each class began.

There was one boy, Peter, who sat at the back. He was not part of Arlene's crowd, though Jill knew he was on the swim team. He had been in a school play last year. Jill had managed a few hellos to him in the hall. Not very casual—they probably had her teeth marks on them. Once she had seen him reading *The Effects of Gamma Rays on Man in the Moon Marigolds* but had not worked up the willpower to ask him about it. She had spent the following two days flogging herself. She had read that play. She had liked that play. She could have asked him about that play. Maybe, just maybe, then . . .

Beside her, Jill saw one of Arlene's admirers pick up a test tube, insert his forefinger. He moved the finger in and out, making small groaning noises. Arlene laughed loudly. As Jill stared intently at her Latin verbs, she felt a flush settle into her pores. There was a sudden silence. She risked a glance at them. They were all staring at her.

Oh, my God! she thought. You can't let your face get any redder. Concentrate on something. Anything. How do you conjugate "My face is on fire," in Latin?

The bell rang. The boys snickered as they left for their seats. Arlene allowed her shoulders to define contempt. For fifty minutes, the two girls were condemned to the distance of one and a half feet.

"Chess," Arlene drawled softly.

"SO WHAT DO YOU WANT to be when you grow up?" Jill asked Cal.

"Aha," said Cal. "Big Brother is checking out how the academic brainwash process is coming along." He moved a knight.

Jill watched his opponent, a thin boy with Bruce Cockburn glasses, stiffen into another dimension.

"I didn't really think of it as a political question," she said.

"It's a political satire," Cal scoffed. "Tell them I want to join the IRA. Or the FLQ."

Jill wrote this down next to *Nurse*. "Good thing I'm not giving names."

"Oh—then I can give you my real goal in life," Cal chirped. "I want to do Minute Rice ads on TV. Try cooking Minute Rice in kiwi juice. Or Javex. It'll taste the same either way." He lowered his voice, breathing heavily. "And how 'bout Darth Vader? I want to play Darth Vader in *Batman Meets Darth Vader*. In their fight to the finish, they could get all tangled up in their cute little lookalike capes and have an identity crisis."

"The Force be with you," sighed Jill. "Why did I ask?" She turned to Cal's opponent. "How 'bout you? What do you want to do with your future? This is for the *Telegraph*."

The boy ripped his gaze from the board. "Huh?"

"I'm doing the survey for the *Telegraph*," Jill repeated. "What do you want to be when you grow up?"

The boy's gaze slid across the classroom walls, unable to get a grasp. "I dunno. A mail carrier? Don't they make a lot?"

"They're privatizing," said Cal. "You'll be working in a back corner of Shoppers Drug Mart. Close to minimum wage."

"Oh," said the boy. "I dunno. Anything."

"I can't write down *Anything*," protested Jill.

"An accountant?" offered the boy.

"Fine," said Jill. She wrote it down.

SHE SAW HIM. He was at the other end of the hallway at his locker, pulling out his sweater—a green sweater. My fave color, Jill thought. This was it. This would be her big chance to start a conversation—a whole real conversation. Think sentences, paragraphs, she encouraged herself. More than just, "Hi."

"Hi," said Jill.

Most of the kids had gone home, and the halls seemed endless and hollow. Peter looked down at her. He was so tall. "Hi. Jill?"

"Yeah. D' you mind if I ask you a question?"

"Sure—shoot." He pulled the sweater on over his head, then leaned against his locker and waited.

His hair was all ruffled and gorgeous. Jill's mind gasped. Her mouth took over. "Well, I'm this year's survey taker for the *Telegraph.*"

"I guess this means I'll be talking to you all year." He was grinning. Jill's heart flopped around in her chest like a landed seal. She laughed.

"Once an issue."

"Sounds good. So, what's the question?"

"I am not responsible for this." This had to be very clear. "Counseling Services wanted us to do it."

"Okay, so I won't sue."

"What do you want to do with your life? What career do you plan to go into?" she asked. Her breath skidded to a halt. Would he hate her for this sheer and absolute waste of his valuable time?

"Oh." He seemed puzzled. "I haven't really thought about it."

"Not even at all?" asked Jill. "Haven't even thought about what you might like to do?"

"Have you?"

"I'd like to host *Morningside,*" she said.

"What's that?"

"It's a radio show, on CBC," she explained.

"Oh." He brightened. "I listen to the Air Farce."

"Oh—that's great!" Jill said, relieved. "Funny show, eh?"

There was a pause. Peter poked at his gym bag with a runner.

"Just name any career," said Jill. "That's good enough. I don't have to say who gave the answer."

Peter looked very serious. "Okay, I've got it." Jill poised her pen. "Cosmetic salesman," he said. "For Revlon."

Laughter elbowed her stomach, but Jill kept her face straight. "Not Cover Girl?"

"Nope," he said. "Definitely Revlon."

They beamed at each another.

"Thanks," said Jill.

"No prob," he replied. "Now, I know what I'm going to do with my life. I can tell my mom and dad. Revlon."

Jill wandered off down the hall, her mind in a fog. Revlon. What a sense of humor. What a guy. What a mouth. Notice those lips?

Jill tripped slightly on a dangling shoelace.

IT WAS WEIRD, this man on the cross and the waterfall. But then, decisions to go through with something were like that. Hopefully, not all of them needed to be as dramatic.

Jill shook her head, trying to get the movie's soundtrack out from between her ears. Sometimes the music kept going round and round and round inside her head until she wished she could unpin an ear like a flap and let the stuff out.

The weirdest thing about the guy on the cross on the CD cover was that if you looked at the picture for a long time, the waterfall began to move. Which was okay because it was supposed to give that illusion. But the guy on the cross stayed still. The guy who was about to die in the middle of all that water stayed absolutely still.

Course he can't move—it's a painting, Jill told herself.

What an awful place to stay, though, halfway to your doom and upside down. She hoped the person who had painted the picture had painted this guy on his cross as already dead, so she was looking at a corpse. That way she did not have to think about him having to die. Jill did not want to experience a mortality crisis every time she picked up the CD.

Food, Jill decided, would be the best thing to help her resolve this optical illusion. She got up to munch out on some ice cream.

JILL SAT on the edge of the bathtub, sweat pants pulled up to her knees. She was staring at her bare legs. The small stubs of hair were at the beginning-to-be-noticeable stage, and she had gym class tomorrow. This meant running around a large drafty room with lots of other bare legs, all goose pimpled. But they would all be well shaven—no scrape marks or shaving scabs about knees or ankles.

Jill only shaved to her knees, where the darker growth seemed to end. "Why do I do this?" she muttered. "Dwayne doesn't have to."

Much as she did not want to admit it, she found her own hairy legs ugly. But why, when it was natural? Well, true, zits were natural, too, and a face on Zit Warp was really ugly. No argument there. Yeah, but zits were tied into hormonal overdrive. Hairy legs were lifelong. Gillette was probably making millions selling razors to eighty-nine-year-old women who were still trying to get rid of all that "unwanted hair."

Jill stared at the wall. She wondered about the identity of the first woman who started shaving and why she started. Her hand clenched the razor. It was probably because some prehistoric football hero had told her to. Jill pondered. Which came first—football or the Shaved Leg Concept?

"I am going to stop shaving my legs," she announced. "And I am going to enter that contest with hairy legs. It's over two months away; that'll give me lots of time to grow monumental hairs. I could even grow split ends on the ends of split ends by then."

Holding the razor aloft, she cried, "There is on this body no unwanted hair! There is only an unwanted razor blade. You are plastic, you are an environmental risk and you are an emotional hazard. Go, therefore, to thy doom."

Jill threw the razor into the garbage. Then she sat and stared at the bathroom walls for a bit. They remained the same shade of yellow. It was a bit deflating, so she got out of the bathtub, pulled her sweat pant legs down from the knees and left the room.

PENNY

Jill knew that phys. ed. was good for her. She hated it anyway. She hated taking off whichever of her black outfits
she happened to be wearing and putting on the blue cotton
uniform. She hated watching all the other girls put on the
same blue cotton uniform. There was a mild comfort in
being able to choose one's own style of running shoes, but
this was usually overridden by Jill's tendency to forget sweat
socks. She generally resorted to turning down her polyester
knee socks so they formed a large circular lump around the
top of her shoes.

It was not that Jill hated exercise. But the concept of running along behind the blue cotton bum ahead of her in a
very large circle around a cold and drafty gym did not appeal
to her. She disliked the unspoken assumption that she should
want to move one ligament, one cell, one nucleus, to the
voice of the current pop star, who, the critics claimed, had
never taken one music lesson in her entire life.

Jill could think of aerobics only as early training for the
military. She had learned to manage the entire rotation of a
volleyball court without leaving one damaging fingerprint on
the volleyball. She was also an expert on the basketball court
and could run around for an entire class looking very busy

and intent. Intent, that is, at avoiding that big round ball thing. Everyone else was so eager to have a go at it, she didn't want to get in their way.

Jill knew she had about one week's grace before her unshaved stubble became apparent to the casual eye. So today should have been a day about as good or bad as any other day that had phys. ed. in it. Except this was the day the class was being marked on their floor routines, and Jill hated floor routines most of all.

For the past several weeks in gym class, Jill had been given an area of eight feet square, and, surrounded by thirty other girls, each in her own area of eight feet square, she had been composing a series of creative and independent moves to the voice of the popular singer who had never taken one music lesson in her entire life. No, Jill reminded herself as she unlocked her locker, it's not one music lesson in her entire family tree.

That is, Jill was supposed to have been coming up with a series of creative and independent moves. Mostly, she ruminated about the coldness of the floor, the hardness of the floor, the coldness of the air, the draftiness of the air, the intensity of the fluorescent lighting, the blueness of her cotton uniform, the smell of her cotton uniform and the ability of the young singer to sing just below every note.

As Jill removed her black sweats in the locker room, she tried to remember the floor routine. She could remember . . . a somersault and . . . another somersault. And somewhere, she remembered a roll, but that could not possibly take up five minutes. She would just have to wing it. Fortunately, all thirty girls were tested at the same time, with Ms. Cottrell's eyes roving over the entire group. Jill hoped she looked a lot like someone else—which might get her a higher mark.

She looked apprehensively at her legs. They still had a slight tinge of August tan. Give them a month and they would be back to the Raw Chicken Drumstick Look. Soon, dark hairs would menace her legs. They would swarm up from her ankles like ants liberated from one of those ant farms.

Jill poked arms and legs into the blue cotton uniform, took an unobtrusive sniff to make sure the armpits had not reached the socially inappropriate stage, folded down her black polyester socks and scuffed her way out to the gym. She experienced her usual brief hesitation at pulling open the door.

I wonder if gyms in California are any warmer, she thought. Then the fluorescent lighting attacked her eyes and shot in after her brain.

She found an eight-by-eight square marked off with masking tape, making sure she was in a well-populated area, and positioned in among the taller girls. They might hide her in their enthusiastic flurry of creative and independent moves. Ms. Cottrell bent over and pushed the play button. Each girl found her starting position. A sidelong glance enabled Jill to copy the girl next to her. The popular singer aimed her voice at the first few notes.

All around Jill, girls started swinging their legs. She attempted moves she hoped would communicate a lotus flower . . . or a Geranium. Whatever. She just moved. Then, she was visited with brilliance. Macaroni—that's what they all looked like. All those legs, up and down and stuck out behind them. They looked like a pot of macaroni at full boil.

Jill did a somersault, wobbled through a roll, then another somersault. She sat still for a moment, feeling a little dizzy.

She decided to do her lotus flower number again.

THE BELL RANG, dismissing science. "Arlene?" Jill asked quickly.

Arlene lounged on her elbow and addressed Jill with her gaze. "What?" She had very white teeth.

"I'm the survey taker for the *Telegraph*, and I wanted to ask you this month's question if that's all right?"

"I guess so."

Jill swallowed. "What are you planning on choosing as your future career?"

"Hah!" snorted Arlene. One of her boys came up behind her.

"What's so funny?" he asked.

"Jill's the *Telegraph* survey taker for the year," said Arlene. "She wants to know what I plan to choose as my future career."

Behind her, the boy twisted one of Arlene's hair strands around his finger. "Did you tell her it isn't legal?" he asked.

Arlene's head snapped away. For a moment, her nostrils tightened, breathing narrow air. Three long hair strands were left between the boy's fingers. Jill felt as if she had suddenly been paralyzed in a position too close to hell.

"I want to be a lawyer, Jill," snapped Arlene. "Write that down." She grabbed her books and swung out past the boy.

Jill thought it would be in her own best interest to appear very caught up in something or other. She concentrated on writing the word *Lawyer* on her list as the boy came around the desk, then leaned over her. Jill could feel his body heat. Oh, my god, she thought, staring down at her list.

"What else you got there, Jill?" His voice slid down her ear. "Let me see your list."

"It's not very interesting," she whispered, sweating.

"Put me down as a doctor. A gynecologist. You know how to spell that?"

"Yeah," said Jill. "I know how to spell it."

"Good." His finger ran down her list. "Millionaire—tough job. Cop—admirable. Missionary—ooooooo. How 'bout you, Jill? What did you write down for yourself?"

Jill tried to keep the shoulder nearest him from crawling up her neck. "I didn't," she said. "I didn't write myself down."

"So, tell me, Jill," drawled the voice in her ear. "Tell Lyle what you want to do with your life."

"A radio announcer," she said finally. Knuckles were cracking all across her brain.

He leaned over her a moment longer, then suddenly straightened and slammed his palm onto the surface of her desk. He watched her stiffen, then walked away.

"Gynecologist," muttered Jill, watching his shape pass out

the door from the corner of her eye. "Remind me never to go to one of those."

"YOU'RE ENTERING the legs competition?!" squealed Deb. She stared at the pink form Jill was filling out on the cafeteria table.

"Yeah," said Jill. "You just have to fill in your name and leave it in the *Telegraph* mailbox. No brain drain here."

"You think you can win?"

There was no need to sift that tone for doubt. "I want to make a point. I'm not entering this competition because I want to torment everyone by forcing them to look at my legs."

"Oh." Deb's braces were strung with celery. "So, what *is* your point?"

"It's not a big deal. I doubt anyone will even notice, really. I'm just going to stop shaving my legs and enter the competition that way."

"Oh, my gaawd!" Deb gaped at her.

"What's the matter?" Jill asked.

"That's gross," said Deb flatly. "Hairy legs are gross."

"Women in Europe don't shave their legs—ever," said Jill. "Or their armpits."

"That's gross," repeated Deb. "Armpits is grosser even."

"Well, it's normal over there."

"But you're not in Europe," pointed out Deb. "You're here."

"Well, so," said Jill, "here's not the only place to be." She thought about this. The statement began to confuse her, possibly more than Deb. She shrugged. "Look, I just don't think everybody has to be the same, that's all." She paused. "And I think it's a stupid competition."

"You're entering something you think is stupid?"

"Well, what am I going to do? Stand in the middle of the audience and shout, 'This is stupid! I am now officially boycotting it!' Nobody's going to listen."

"Well, are you going to get up on stage and say it's stupid?" Deb gnawed ferociously on her celery.

"I dunno. Deb, this isn't Drama Of The Week or nuthin'. I think I'll just do whatever competitors are supposed to do—walk around the stage, I guess. Only my legs will be hairy, that's all."

Deb squinted, looking deflated. "I think they'll just think you're stupid," she said, thoughtfully.

Jill sighed. "Yeah, probably. But anybody who has a brain at all might think something about it."

"I doubt it," said Deb. "You're complicated, Jill."

"Don't you ever wonder about where it's all going, Deb?" Jill asked. "Don't you ever think—"

"Sure I think!" snapped Deb, waving her stick of celery.

"No, no, that's not what I meant," said Jill. "Oh, forget it. You want to enter?"

"Oh, my gaawd!" said Deb.

SOMETIMES JILL THOUGHT she could feel the hairs on her legs growing. Their points were rough, like small bristles. And they were ugly—no two ways about it. All this dark stuff, crowding onto her skin. Maybe, she figured, leg hair had something to do with memory retention. That was why women had ended up as housewives for so long. All the stuff they took in school, like physics and math—especially trig— maybe all that stuff was contained in leg hair. All these years, women had been shaving off important data. No wonder they didn't have any of the top jobs. No wonder men wanted them to shave the hair off.

The days her hairs grew especially long, those days, Jill decided, she learned the most. She would concentrate on growing a wolf pack of fiendishly brilliant hairs in science class.

AS SHE SAT, chin on knees, and watched *The Mission* video, it occurred to Jill that the Guaraní did not really want churchtype salvation. Sure, they learned the church music, but they loved to sing. Maybe, as they had tied the first Jesuit priest to that cross, they thought the priest was kind of stupid. There sure weren't any Guaraní floating down the river on a cross. They seemed to be quite happy singing and living their environmentally friendly lifestyle.

But maybe, Jill thought, that was because the Guaraní just wanted to live. Maybe they didn't get hung up on any of this religious idealism stuff. Course, they all got shot in the end, anyway. His Eminence, Mega Creep from Europe, got rid of them. His Eminence didn't let any of this idealism crap screw up his brain.

The priests who came from Europe weren't used to this freedom with . . . well, with everything. The freedom of the jungle got to them so much, maybe scared them so much that they wanted to die, wanted to ride down the river on an idea.

Thinking is a drain on personal resources, Jill decided. She turned her brain off.

JILL FELT four-dimensional as she entered the next *Telegraph* meeting. Everyone watched her breathe. Rob howled, then broke off into a series of syncopated yips.

"Okay, so Jill's here," Ewald sighed. "Let's call this meeting to order. Rob, please."

Rob quieted down but continued to smirk at Jill.

"Swallow a UFO?" she asked.

"To order!" Ewald snapped. His eyes made a vague fix on the ceiling, and he struggled with an earlobe. "Jill, your name is on one of these entry forms."

There was another low howl.

"Shut up, Rob," murmured Ewald. "Jill, why is your name on one of these entry forms?"

"Well, what?" demanded Jill. That alien was using her mouth again. "I've got legs. Can't I enter?"

"It makes it a little difficult, Jill." Ewald focused on his buttons. "You are on the *Telegraph* committee."

"I didn't vote for it," said Jill. "Besides, there are no rules against it. Anybody can enter."

"I have this . . . well . . . this feeling that you have a motive," said Ewald. "It sounds kind of feminist to me."

"Feminists don't have legs?" said Jill.

"I'm repeating myself," groaned Ewald. "I hate repeating myself."

Jill felt like a terrorist. "What's your point, Ewald?"

Ewald had exposed a large region of grey tee shirt. "This event is sponsored by us. I don't want any problems."

"I'm not planning any," said Jill. "I've got an idea for the next survey."

Ewald's eyelids hovered suspiciously over his gaze. "What?"

"How 'bout: What other object do legs resemble? We could point out how funny legs really look. An answer could be: A piece of spaghetti!"

"No," sighed Ewald. "We are not asking that for the survey question. I have one here for you. This one's from Student Council."

"What is it this time?" asked Jill.

"They want to know how much kids would be willing to pay for a good band at a dance," said Ewald. "All they want to know is dollars and cents."

"Boring." Jill slumped forward until her chin met the desktop, then concentrated on creating a film of moisture on the varnished surface with her breath.

"And look, I don't want to have to edit out all of the pointless silly answers this time, okay, Jill? You get a silly answer, don't write it down. Nobody wants to hear it."

"I have a question," said Jill, still staring at the desktop. It made her cross-eyed, but the meeting looked more interesting this way.

"About the survey?" sighed Ewald.

"No, sports announcements. I don't see why you have to announce me as part of the chess team."

"That's not *Telegraph* business," said Ewald. "Talk to Rob about it. He handles sports for the sports committee. What's our next issue, Beth?"

"Layout," said Beth.

Under the desk, Jill twisted her fingers into pretzels. Yeah, right, she was going to talk to *Rob* about it. And what was the matter with her survey question? How much would you pay to get into a school dance!

She would run her survey. She would run his, but she would run her own, too. If she had to, she would publish it herself—a black market issue.

Watching the desktops cross and recross in front of her eyes, Jill zippered the thought carefully closed.

DWAYNE'S SUPPER-TABLE GLARE hacked away at her over his liver and onions. "Do you mind not ramming your eyes down my throat?" Jill asked. "I'm eating."

"You had to do it, didn't you?"

"Had to do what?" Jill asked in her airy voice.

"You know what." Dwayne poked at his liver. She knew he was trying to decide how to get it down his throat without tasting any of it. So was she.

"I don't," mused their father. He enjoyed liver.

"Neither do I," contributed their mother. She had cooked the liver.

Dwayne tapped his fork, flipping a few green beans off his plate. "The football team and the *Telegraph* are sponsoring a competition in the middle of December. And Jill is against the competition. And she's"—Dwayne slowed down to emphasize each word—"going to go into the competition just to bug everybody. It pisses me off."

"What's the competition?" asked their father.

Dwayne shoved his mouth full of potatoes without answering.

"Jill?" asked her father. He was in Noninterference Information Seeking Mode.

"Oh, it's this competition about who has the best legs in school," said Jill. "Could you pass the HP Sauce please?"

Jill's father raised his eyebrows. "Not exactly your type of competition."

"I got legs," said Jill. "They work fine."

"Sounds good to me," said Jill's mother. "Here's the HP Sauce, dear."

Dwayne glared at Jill. You are a pain in the ass, his eyes said, and I am going to make your life as hard for you as you make mine for me.

Jill blinked delicately at him and nibbled on a tiny, HP-drenched speck of liver.

JILL WAS TRYING not to think about penises. Again. She gave up trying to memorize the function of the kidney and spleen, and flipped through her health textbook. There it was—the black-and-white line drawing.

Why did they call it a wiener? Looked more like an old-fashioned water faucet. And how come it changed shape like that?

She lay on her back and tried to imagine what it would feel like to have something like that between her legs, then inside of her. She imagined. And she imagined. The abstract penis did not do much for her, so she wrinkled her nose and flopped back on her side. She observed the textbook again. She had kissed a few guys. Her junior high boyfriend had been pretty good at it. Thinking about kissing made her lips tickle just under the surface. A slight sweat broke out all over her.

She did not get it—about penises. They looked like a disaster, kind of silly, like an empty sock. She wished they did not exist. She had a feeling that if they all vanished, life would be a lot simpler.

The kissing could stay. That would be all right.

JILL GLOPPED hot oatmeal into a bowl, layered it with brown sugar, then repeated the process. She poured on cold milk. Then she played hit and run with her tongue and the too-hot-to-eat conglomeration. Mom and Dad had gone to work. Dwayne did not exist. She grabbed her books, shoved herself into her windbreaker, stepped out and locked the back door.

"What the hell are you trying to do?"

Revise that nonexistence clause. Dwayne leaned against

the back fence. Jill felt alarm jerk inside of her and tried to keep her face very still.

"Smartass," he continued. "That's how come you turn people off. You're always trying to make them look stupid, y' know. You always got some smartass answer for everything."

"Maybe if you just *asked* me a question, instead of always attacking me with it." Jill tried to swallow the tremble in her voice. "Exactly which one of my activities d' you want to know about?"

His voice quickened. "Look, I don't get you. I don't get how you got this way." He walked back and forth along the green mesh fence. Prowling, Jill thought. Suddenly he swung at it with his fist, so that the fence clattered against the posts in waves. There was a pause that seemed violent, straining between them. The vibrations of the fence diminished.

Dwayne stared at the ground as Jill stared at his face. There was a giant hole in her head where thought usually lurked. Briefly, his eyes met hers. They were an unavoidable blue. Whenever they caught her directly, something inside her began to hurt.

"I want to know why you're entering that competition."

Jill placed her palm against the side of the house. The old brick was cold, clammy. Did she really have a reason? Hair on legs—was that really a reason?

"I don't know why."

"What d' you mean, you don't know why?"

"Anyone can enter. What's the big deal with *me?*"

Dwayne stared at his left runner. They had been strangers for so long, Jill thought. Why the sudden interest?

Then, I want you to know, she thought fiercely. I want you to understand.

"I don't want to see you do it, Jill," he mumbled. He would not look up and began hacking at the grass with his heel.

"Why not?" This was different, this mood of his. He wasn't wearing his football uniform now. She thought she could

46

feel him finger his thoughts, try to fit them to the English language. Were there too many words, or not enough? He looked up and away. His lips made thin hard lines around the sounds.

"They'll think you're a slut."

The words slammed into her face, and Jill swallowed. So that was it. A slut for a sister. Finally, she could actually affect him, damage his cosmic reputation.

"I think it's a goddamn stupid competition," she said. "And I'm going to try and screw it up for all of you as much as I can."

She whirled and pushed away from him through air that seemed suddenly thick. She was halfway to school before the other possibility hit her. Maybe he was concerned about *her* reputation. Jill walked faster, trying to leave that *if only* behind. If only he had found that sentence, the one he gave up on, and had gotten what he had really meant across the space between them.

JILL'S LATIN CLASS was composed of the nerd species. As an option, only those who had grey cells to waste took it. Mostly, it consisted of memory work. As far as viable conversation went, the only thing Jill figured she could ask was *"Ubi est canis?"* as in "Where is the dog?" Or, for variety, she could throw in, "Where is the slave girl?"

As she climbed the stairs to the language and history floor, Jill hiked her binder closer to her bent elbow. It was the third floor, closest to the clouds. Latin was the first door on the right. She chose her regular desk next to the window. A wide selection of desks was always available because only ten students had given way to the manic urge to take Latin. This meant no one had to sign a name on a little square on a seating plan, promising to sit there all year. Jill crossed her left ankle over her right knee, noticed the stubble on her ankle, pushed down her black jean leg and set her foot back down on the floor.

Greg Sacuta came in loudly and took his seat at the back,

then started with his voice. It reminded Jill of a cruise missile test because it destroyed all of the natural auditory environment. Greg put his voice on repeat a lot, especially when informing them, once again, that he had taken this course as Preparation For Law Studies.

Jill had taken Latin for interest. She did not broadcast her reason in stereo or in whispers. It was her secret.

Mr. Sinclair huddled behind his desk. He was a victim, and everything about him begged you notice the fact. His shoulders slumped. His voice had an apologetic curve. He stood very still and spoke quietly, as if to take up as little attention as possible. His smile was a question mark. He squinted at students, estimating their mood, then slid sideways up from behind his desk into the range of greater visibility and began to murmur.

Jill usually whittled away large amounts of class time observing the smoking elite out on the sidewalks. Deeply involved with her analysis of their interactions, it took Jill ten minutes to notice that Mr. Sinclair's fly was down. Deb finally hissed the information into her ear. Jill checked it out immediately.

Yes, it was true. Mr. Sinclair's cords were buttoned under the sad-lump stomach, but the fly had pulled apart, exposing light-brown jockey shorts. Jill wondered what to do. She looked at her classmates. They had all noticed. She could tell by the unusual interest that lurked in their eyes. Greg leaned back in his seat, grinning furiously.

Mr. Sinclair requested they complete a full conjugation of ten verbs, then slipped out of the classroom. Greg laughed. The sound scraped at Jill like a scouring pad.

"Okay," said Greg. "Everybody listen up. When he comes back, this is what we do. I drop my pencil. I go down to pick it up. When I come back up, everybody in sync, here—you look at his face, you look at his fly, you look at his face, you look at his fly. Three times."

Some of the kids laughed. If graphed with the general school population, Greg was of minimal importance, but as a relative nonnerd in Latin nerddom, he ruled. Jill sat on the

48

edge of the conversation, staring down the precipice of different thinking. She felt words signifying disapproval or disagreement grow in her throat, but they would not come out. She sweated, wanting to speak. C'mon Jill, enunciate, her brain howled.

Mr. Sinclair walked back in. Rats, thought Jill. You stupid man. She had hoped he'd made a discrete exit to zip up the fly, but obviously he had not.

Nobody had conjugated. Mr. Sinclair expressed weak disappointment and suggested they begin work. To his amazement, their heads bent, as if on cue. For once, it was his cue.

Then Greg dropped his pencil. Jill felt her head turn sideways with the others and watched him pick it up. Mr. Sinclair stood beside his desk, arms wrapped about his chest in their usual cradling gesture. As Jill watched, the eyes around her traveled face to fly, then repeated the motion twice, unzipping Mr. Sinclair's guts. A few snickered.

Mr. Sinclair realized something was up. Confusion ran mouse tracks across his face. His smile questioned. Jill shoved her voice out of her throat. "Mr. Sinclair," she rasped, "I've got the verbs, if you want to hear them."

His gratitude was frightening. Jill read each word slowly. Fifteen minutes to go. Ten verb conjugations could not claim so much time no matter how she dragged it out. She felt Greg throwing eye grenades at her back. The hole at Mr. Sinclair's crotch seemed to be widening. She looked at the clock. Still ten minutes to go.

Greg dropped his pencil again, bent to pick it up. "Geez, Greg," said Jill. "What's the problem with the pencil, today?"

Greg's eyes obliterated her face. "Mr. Sinclair," he drawled, "your fly is down."

Nervously, the class laughed. Mr. Sinclair's face lost a tenuous grip on its expression and got all twisted up. He turned and shifted himself out of the room, his bones moving awkwardly in their fat. Some of the class forced their laughter to louder tones.

Greg grinned without amusement. Jill thought she could feel his gaze briefly poke at the mole on the side of her neck. She swiveled, facing Deb. "You didn't do it?" she asked. "You didn't do that looking at his fly bit?"

"Um, yeah," said Deb. "You gotta admit—it was kinda funny. Sinclair's a lost cause. He'll have a nervous breakdown in a year or so, and they'll get a decent teacher in here. He should work in a flower shop or something. I hear he's gay, anyways."

The bell rang. The situation was dismissed.

JILL HURRIED into the closest washroom. She ducked into a cubicle and slid her sweat pants down. A red blotch glared up at her. She sat down on the toilet and leaned a hot face against the metal barrier. So that's where all those weird feelings had come from in Latin.

Greg would make her pay. Who was Mr. Sinclair, anyway? So what if he's gay? Can't he be gay? Law against that?

Jill ripped the toilet paper off the roll and wiped the stain on her underwear. No spare change. She would have to run home. It was only two blocks. She could manage it.

Why'd it have to show up four days early? Next month, Jill decided, she would mark a two-week margin in bright red on the calendar: Warning—DO NOT BE BRAVE ON THESE DAYS!

Sliding out the bathroom door, Jill hoped nobody would smell the blood.

JILL WAS LISTENING again to *The Mission* soundtrack. Dwayne had thrown his sweater over his head and gone to his room in search of earphones and something very different to listen to. Her mother was engrossed in the *Globe and Mail*.

The soundtrack began with the voices of the Guaraní singing church music. Jill studied the pink, blue, brown, white waterfall on the CD cover. There was a parallel here, she decided. The voices were like the waterfall . . . and like life, she supposed—always moving and changing shape. She wished she knew exactly why and how the music took her through her Big Bawl And Weep Scenario.

The voices were painfully beautiful. They cut fine lines into Jill's awareness. When the CD had played itself out, Jill had that intense feeling again inside that there was meaning to existence, One Big Truth To Being Alive. She did not have the words to describe it, but she felt it. Sighing, she blew her nose.

FRIDAY AFTERNOON was deceptively benign. Clipboard hugged to her nonexistent bosom, Jill meandered along the sidewalk, breathing in the rich October smell of leaves.

If I made up the answers to this survey, she wondered, would anybody notice? If I made them all around the same amount, a reasonable amount . . . What if I said seven dollars and fifty cents? Student Council would be happy with that. That's probably what they'd charge anyways. Oh, ask a couple of people to be on the safe side.

Halfway through the late afternoon class, Rob's voice had nosed its way out of the PA, dialoguing with each individual's secret pocket of school spirit and guilt. There was a big game today. He gave them the usual line: "Need your support. Need you to win."

Bull crappola, Jill thought. Then she decided to view the game as a journalistic opportunity. After school, she headed off toward Exhibition Park. Maybe she had ignored the existence of the football team to this point in her academic career, but she did have a survey to complete.

The school crowd had shaped itself into a bell curve along the sideline. As Jill wandered over, a shout went up. The crowd became suddenly taller. Jill meandered along the sideline to a goal post, where she could get a view of the playing field.

They were out there, so far downfield they looked like colorful little macaroons with helmets and legs. Jill began to giggle. It was beyond her. The grass was dry so she sat down. There seemed to be a lot of running around, some shouting and grunting—a bunch of guys in blue and a bunch of guys in red. At least in figure skating, Jill knew what was going on.

The cheerleaders jumped up and jogged to the front of the crowd. Each girl's legs spread out to form a triangle with the ground.

Jill's eyes narrowed. Her theory on cheerleaders was that Ms. Cottrell chose whoever fit the uniforms most accurately. The girls' shoulders filled out the little blue outfits, their legs creating strong sure lines to give their skirts their correct prim flip. They were all in time, in stride. Pompoms waved in perfect unison.

"Go team, go team, go team, go team," the girls chanted.

Jill hated cheerleaders. More, even, than football. Soccer didn't have cheerleaders. Baseball didn't have cheerleaders. Even hockey didn't have cheerleaders. What was it about football? She watched the line of girls. They were so sure, moving exactly in line with one another, as if no out-of-step action was expected or desired. It was as if to desire an out-of-step step or thought was ridiculous.

Legs kicked, swung, swiveled. The girls made a half circle, facing the crowd and chanting. The benevolent October sun fell on their positive faces, their earnest arms and legs. Mostly legs. Strong legs. Legs that worked hard. Competent. Obedient. Five pairs of them. And they moved together. In step. In thought. Shaved.

School spirit. These girls were full of it.

The cheerleaders had the crowd wound up now. The crowd pulsed with the chant, clapping. Jill stared at them. A few minutes ago, these kids had been individuals, in groups of scattered conversations, the game a part of their peripheral vision. Now they were one. One chant. One handclap.

So what? Jill asked herself. They're idiots. That doesn't make it your problem.

But then what was she bracing her body against? Suddenly, she knew. Inside. It was inside. She could feel it there. The pulse of the crowd had her heart, was pounding it out. Her heart beat to the rhythm of the clapping hands, the strident mouths. The energy pulsed in her arms, her legs. This is Me Warp, Jill thought. Get a grip.

The girls swiveled again, facing the game. They had the crowd. They had the sun. They had their glorious boys in blue.

Jill saw her brother, number eleven. The shirt was perpetually draped somewhere in the laundry room. It was the only way she could have identified Dwayne on the field amidst all those oversized outlines. She watched number eleven run, sidestep, then ram himself against a red form. They crashed to the ground.

With a start, Jill realized she was chewing her gum in rhythm to the clapping. It would have been melodramatic, pretentious, to admit that she wanted to cry. Her eyes stung, became wet. Here she was, as usual, not getting along with the others and hating everyone, including herself, for it. Jill decided to go home. She would make up answers to the survey on the way, maybe add a few real ones later.

Walking away from the game, Jill felt the crowd's chant diminish in her ears, her head, muscles, gut. But her legs. Her legs. She was walking in time to that far-off chant.

With a few skips, Jill broke into a run.

THE SECOND TOURNAMENT was being held in Arthur, about an hour's drive from Guelph. Mr. Fizell's car smelled of old newspapers. Once again, Jill sat in the front seat. She made sure she dragged an answer to the second survey from each boy on the team. Her quota was twenty-five answers. Three down, twenty-two to go.

"Nothing," Cal replied promptly. "There are no good bands today. They all died in the Seventies."

The chess tournament was held in the school library. There were thirty-seven competitors, including one girls team from a Catholic school.

Jill approached them with mixed feelings. A lot of giggles came from their general vicinity. Two of the four left for the washroom to rearrange their faces. The other two said hello, then walked around the tables, examining the boards that had been set up. Jill shrugged. Don't be sexist, she told herself. Why should they want to talk to you anymore than anyone else?

The games had no time limit. As she sat down for her first match, Jill's mind felt energetic, shoveling thoughts in all directions. She concentrated on moving her players forward, leaving one rook to defend the back row. In her mind, her opponent deteriorated to a vague concept.

Soon her eyes had burnt themselves out, running back and forth across the board. A blizzard filled her brain, turning its lower section to sludge. She took a deep breath and looked up.

A large quiet crowd surrounded them. She looked about the library. There were no other games in progress—they had all finished. Cal sat on a nearby table, swinging one leg. Mr. Fizell stroked his smile.

"Why doesn't she see it?" someone whispered.

Jill stiffened. What was she missing this time? She looked back at the board, then at Mr. Fizell.

"Take your time, Jill," he said. "Just take your time."

Jill looked and looked. Her opponent made his move. He was hunched over, worry having a field day with his forehead. She must be doing all right! The realization came as a complete surprise.

Then she glanced at the clock. They had been playing for an hour and a half!

"It's so obvious," someone else whispered.

If I had enough energy, Jill thought, I'd become slightly hysterical. What am I doing right?

She plodded from possibility to possibility. Then she looked at her opponent, noticed his glance flick nervously to his right corner and followed it there. Of course, a possible check! She moved her rook. About her, the air relaxed. She saw Cal half smile. Mr. Fizell rocked on his heels.

"Check?" she asked.

Without a word, the boy jerked himself up from his seat and away from the table. Everyone else drifted away. Jill didn't understand. Had he given her a default? Wearily, she pushed back her chair and wandered to a nearby window, then stared out at the falling rain. After a while, she found she was able to distinguish one falling raindrop from another. She wandered back to the board and looked at it.

Checkmate! No wonder he had left. She had won her first game. It would have been nice to be able to say honestly that she had been even slightly aware of the win when it had happened. And where was that *Kitchener-Waterloo Record* photographer now?

Jill bombed her next game in ten minutes. "My brain is hyperventilating," she told Mr. Fizell.

"That's okay," he said. "You did really well the first time."

At another table, one of the girls was giggling. "What a good move," she kept telling her opponent. Jill lost her third game in a respectable amount of time. Cal won all three of his games. Their team placed second overall. As they drove back to Guelph, Jill curled into the comfort of her first win.

THERE THEY WERE, all of a sudden, interrupting her graph of negative integers. They were lined up on a stage in her head, a long row of penises in frilled skirts, doing the Can Can. First they dangled, then they did an erection. Then they performed another dangle and another erection, backed up by the Boston Pops Orchestra in tuxedos and evening dresses, concentrating very seriously on an intricate and complicated arrangement of the Can Can musical score.

This cannot be happening, thought Jill, sitting up on her bed. This is not normal.

"I hate this," she said aloud. "I hate this." She threw her pencil onto the floor. She sulked.

" . . . NEARING THE END of the playoffs and need your support. Come on out and show your school spirit."

More of Rob's dribble, Jill thought, doodling on the edge

of her Duotang. What was that? She examined her art work more closely. It was one of those penises! Furiously, she scribbled it out. How had that crawled out of the end of her pen?

" . . . and congratulations to our chess team, which placed second in a tournament this past weekend. Congratulations especially to Jill Gilbert, who defeated her opponent after a strenuous ninety minutes of head-to-head combat. And that's it for sports. Remember the football game."

Jill shaped her mouth in a smile for the approving looks of her classmates and homeroom teacher. "I lost my second game in ten minutes," she announced loudly. "Cal won all three of his games."

Everyone looked away again. That was better, she thought. More honest. Cynicism stuck like dry oatmeal in her throat.

"SO IT TOOK YOU ninety minutes to win a chess game, eh, Jill?"

The two hemispheres of Jill's brain slammed together. She knew that voice. She had secretly dubbed its owner Miss Popular Ass but had kept this to herself, possessing some instinct for survival. Karen Ezacko. Jill tried to keep out of her way. Three or four other girls followed her around like lemmings on steroids. They were always on the lookout for a victim.

Jill moved in closer to her gym locker and quickly buttoned up her uniform. It was better to leave as little as possible exposed. "Yeah, it took ninety minutes." Her voice cracked. Sure, Jill. Advertise your nerves.

"Didn't know lumberjacks played chess," said a lemming.

It was happening, Jill thought. It was starting to kick into gear.

"Y' know, Jill, they got razors on sale at the BiWay," said another lemming. "'Bout a quarter each. Need a loan?"

Jill wanted to put her right foot on a bench so that she could fold down her sock, but her shoe seemed to be stuck to the floor. She thought she should look busy, perhaps casually busy. Reach for the locker, Jill, she thought. This movement will communicate to these Rabid Female Terminator II types that everything is normal, functional.

But now her arm refused to move, and this presented a problem. How could she carry off her No This Is Not The End Of The World Routine without joints? And why was she letting her stomach turn this into such a big deal? Hairs had been devouring her legs for three weeks now. Only bean sprouts accumulated size more quickly.

"I bet she's got hairy boobs."

The words had an exact nastiness to them. Jill did have black hairs growing around her nipples, and these she continued to cut, so close she often drew blood. Her face suddenly red, Jill felt the air move in and clamp down around her.

Then, with a small mental explosion, Jill realized something she had forgotten. Each leg hair contained a microscopic nuclear missile. Their secret control button was at the tip of her tongue, and all she had to do was press it against her teeth. Immediately, all those little missiles would shoot from her legs and find their trajectory, straight for Karen's brain. No, that was a target too small for reason—better aim for her burgeoning attitude.

Jill opted for the luxury of mercy, curling the tip of her tongue back from her teeth. She breathed and found she was now able to lift her feet, one by one, and fold down her socks. Closing her locker door, she clicked the combination lock shut.

Jill felt very calm. Her eyes had the determination and strength of lighthouse beams. She could deal with that rat Karen with her little finger. As Jill turned, her eyes swung around, focused on the place her opponent stood waiting.

There was no one there. She stared at the empty locker room. Everyone must have gone to the gym. When had they all left? Shit. She was probably late!

Shit.

She scurried to the gym door.

Shit.

She grabbed the door handle, hesitated.

Shit.

Bracing herself for the fluorescent lighting, she entered.

ARLENE WAS ABSENT. The bell had rung, and the space above her stool had not filled with negative energy. Jill felt her own aura change from a bleak grey to an enthusiastic yellow. She would have to join another group to do the sodium chloride experiment.

"Jill."

It was Peter. Those lips—what were they saying? Words were coming out of his mouth. Consciousness was sliding out of Jill's grasp like a greased pig. He was so tall. "Hi," she managed.

"D' you want to be my partner for this experiment?" he asked. "Amil isn't here today."

Yes, yes, yes, yes, yes, Jill's mind squealed. "Sure."

"I'll get the stuff." He left to get the equipment.

God, he looks good in blue. Jill made a fierce attempt to grab control of her mind. The chemical name for water. H_2O. H_2O. Conjugate. *Ancilla, ancillam, ancillae, ancillas* . . .

"Here we are," said Peter. He began to set up the Bunsen burner. "How come I haven't gotten the survey question this month?"

"I'm making most of it up—the answers, I mean," said Jill.

He laughed. "Serious?"

"Do you know what they're making me ask?"

"No."

"How much money would you pay for a school dance if they got a good band?"

"Well, that would depend on the band," he said.

"Exactly."

"So you're making it all up, eh?"

When he grinned, her knees experienced a chemical change. They melted to H_2O.

Peter set up the Bunsen burner and filled the test tubes. "Why don't you graph? Oh, by the way—congratulations on your chess game."

Jill thought she would put this comment into the Guinness Book of World Compliments. "Thanks," she glowed.

"Okay," said Peter. "First reading is one point three centimeters."

Jill logged it. Lucky we're not graphing my stomach, she thought.

"Are you a friend of Arlene's?" Peter asked.

"Uh, no," said Jill. "Just luck I got to be her science partner."

"Bad luck," grunted Peter. "It's two point seven, now."

"You know her very well?"

"Yeah, really," he snorted. He saw her relief and grinned. "Three point five," he said. "That's what I'd give Arlene out of ten. On a good day. But, yeah, that's the reading, too."

They watched the test tube.

"You should join the swim team," Peter suggested.

"I'm a lousy swimmer."

"Oh."

Once again, silence shouldered its way into their conversation.

"Three point eight," said Peter. "Boy, if this gets much higher, we won't be able to call it The Arlene Experiment."

Jill began to feel cheerful about Amil's absence. And she hoped Arlene had died.

"Four point two," Peter said.

DWAYNE HAD FORGOTTEN his lunch again. Jill hated this because her mother made her bring his lunch over to the football practice. Jill figured Dwayne was old enough to suffer the consequences of lunch bags slipping his mind. Slippery area, that mind. Unfortunately, her mother was able to see more potential in the wasteland that existed between Dwayne's ears and figured it should be fed on a regular basis. Cultivated, even.

Jill was disgusted. She told herself she hated the smell and the noise that emerged from the boys locker room, but it was the inexplicable feelings rocketing around her lower abdomen that she really wanted to avoid. She did not have a strong grip on her hormones, and she knew it. She would have preferred to channel her energy toward an idolization of Einstein, Plato, even Mr. Somayaji, her math teacher. But instead, her hormones were more interested in these guys who could hardly stuff their egos into their football uniforms. Priority Warp here, Jill told herself. You'll turn into a red neon sign if anyone notices you. And keep your eyes off the lower areas.

Some of the team were coming out into the hall. Jill saw her brother carrying equipment. "Dwayne," she called out. "You forgot your lunch." She waved it in the air.

Dwayne swung around. "Hey, you guys," he said. "Here's one of our contestants. Did you know my sister entered The Lovely Legs Competition?"

Panic shoved its way up Jill's chest. The entire team must be there, turning in her direction. One of the guys dropped to his knees and started crawling toward her.

"Legs, legs," he chanted. "Let me see those legs."

Jill threw the lunch bag straight at Dwayne's face. Hard. She tried to move away, but her way was blocked. Most of the team was down on its knees chanting, "Legs, legs." They were hemming her in. A blush flowed through her, acidic, burning in its intensity.

"Marry me," someone called out. They were all shouting it. "Marry me, marry me!" Turning, Jill hid her face against a hallway locker. Its cold surface pushed back against her. Someone's face bumped the back of her knee, then another.

There was someone else, pushing and shoving through the guys on the floor, an older voice yelling at them to stand up and stop being such idiots. The guys quieted. She could hear them getting to their feet. Coach Booth was at her ear. "Are you all right?"

Jill did not want to see his face. She pushed by him and

ran quickly down the hall. Behind her, she felt silence thicken and fill the space between the walls.

AT SUPPER, Dwayne hovered over his pork chops, apologetic. "Look, Jill, it was just a joke. What'd you get so upset about?"

Refusing to look at him, Jill took her plate and left the table. "I will eat in my room," she said over her shoulder. She sat at her desk and poked at the food. She was still shaking. How had that happened, in the hall? What had happened to that group of boys? It was almost as if someone had pushed a button, and they had all been jerked into action at the same time.

"Did I think they'd tear off my clothes and rape me right there in the hallway?" she asked herself aloud. "No."

Her answer sounded decisive, even astounding, to her. "No," she repeated more quietly. It was something else. "It was as if I could've been anyone. Any girl."

She had never before felt so impersonal, defaced. It scared her.

Her father knocked on the door. "Hi," his head said, sticking itself around the half-open door. "How're my pork chops?"

A smile poked at the corners of Jill's mouth. "Good, Dad. You're getting real professional with Shake 'n Bake."

"So long as they're well done," he said, bringing in the rest of his body. "Can't have a medium rare pork chop—death and all that stuff." He sat down on her bed and twiddled his thumbs. "Sounds like you got treated pretty rough today."

"Well, they didn't hurt me."

"No, but they were demeaning." She could feel her father's anger. It made her suddenly want to start crying in relief. "Nobody should be treated that way," he added. "Are you sure you want to enter that legs competition?"

"Well, there's kind of a point to it," Jill explained. "I was going to stop shaving my legs. It's still two months to go and, well, y' see, make a point that way."

"Oh," grinned her father. "Is your mother involved in this?"

"No," said Jill uncertainly. "Well, the shaving my legs or not shaving my legs was my idea. I could wear army boots or something."

Her father laughed. "So, my daughter takes after her mother. Sounds okay to me." He sobered. "Those boys shouldn't have done what they did. It's hard at any age, but especially at yours, to stand up for what's right. Probably each one of those boys is ashamed of himself now. Your brother feels pretty bad. Not that I'm excusing them, of course."

Although Jill was not at all convinced about the ability of any teenage football player to experience remorse, she, at that moment, loved her father very, very much. "Dad," she said, "isn't empathy located in the frontal lobe? Don't you think it'd be shattered to very small bits by the number of hours they spend running headfirst into sandbags?"

"Ah," observed her father. "A little bit of the fighting spirit returns. Shall I go speak to your principal?"

"Please don't," said Jill. "Thanks. But from now on, Dwayne takes his own lunch. And if he forgets it, well, he can borrow someone else's Twinkies."

JILL REPLAYED the movie scenes with His Eminence. What made him different? she wondered. How come he didn't end up as a martyr?

He hardly ever moved. He just sat watching the Guaraní sing. Or he walked with as little movement as possible around the Jesuit mission.

Maybe he knew that was the only way to survive, Jill thought. With all those voices shifting and moving around him, maybe he figured he had to keep himself absolutely still so they wouldn't pick him up and carry him along. That way, they wouldn't change any of his ideas, which had been to sell all the Guaraní off in the first place.

He must have had to hold himself so still he never

breathed, Jill thought. He would've had to hold his thoughts as still inside his brain as that first priest had held his body while the Guaraní tied him to the cross.

Pretty heavy duty, Jill told herself. The reality of this intelligence scared her. She decided to temporarily avoid it and took herself off to the kitchen to find some barbecue chips.

TIME YAWNED and another week crawled out between its teeth. The afternoon blinked and rubbed its eyes. Jill was rolling her pencil between her fingers. Good ol' HB, she thought. Her chair was bothering her butt. Rob was giving her all the peripheral vision he could manage. He smirked. Mentally, she sicked her deadly leg hairs on him.

"This won't be a long meeting," said Ewald. "Deadline for everything is tomorrow, right?"

Nobody answered. Ewald sighed.

"Rob, are you ready?" he asked.

"Yup," said Rob.

"Beth?"

"Yes," said Beth.

"How 'bout you, Jill?"

"I only got one answer," Jill warned.

Ewald took a deep breath. "What does that mean?"

"Everybody said, 'I dunno, depends on the band.'" She felt a mild triumph. "And I have a better survey question for next time."

"And what might that be?" Ewald's energy rose one notch above the sigh level.

"Do you think the legs competition is sexist?"

The eyes of everyone around her, like venetian blinds, suddenly closed.

"Well, why not?" she demanded. "It's an open-ended question. They can say what they want."

"I think it's negative," said Beth. "Kids don't care about that kind of thing."

Silent, Rob balanced himself on two chair legs, watching.

Apathy sure was trendy. Their lack of response did in Jill's series of prepared questions. Why don't I quit? she wondered. I could make a scene and walk out. It could be fun.

"Leave it alone," Ewald sighed. "We talked about this last time. The next survey has to do with the cafeteria menu."

"Well, can I just write an article, then?" asked Jill.

"You're the survey taker," said Ewald. "That's your job. And the budget won't allow it. We can't afford the space."

"I think this is more important than the survey," protested Jill.

Ewald shrugged. "*You* think," he pointed out.

Yes, I do, Jill thought. Then she recalled her idea about the black market newspaper issue. She still needed this bunch.

"Renita, are you ready?" Ewald sighed.

SLAVE TRADER

The last few social history classes had tackled the topic of rape. A student had just completed a presentation on its effects upon the victim. As she resumed her seat, the teacher, Ms. Thiessen, said, "I want to discuss the results of the survey we took last class. As you remember, the question was: 'If the boy pays for the date, does he have the right to expect sex from his partner?' Eleven out of sixteen male students checked off yes. Out of the eleven female students, five checked yes. I want to throw this open for discussion. Any comments?"

Jill opened her mouth and some words stomped out. "So if the girl pays, does she have a right to expect sex from the guy?"

There were snickers. Jill heard Dwayne clear his throat. Now that the football season was over, he was playing first string on the basketball team. It had not brought the two of them any closer.

He hates me, she thought.

One of the boys at the back of the room scoffed, "I've never gone out with a girl who paid for a date. I wouldn't let her."

"Why not?" asked Ms. Thiessen.

"What if she wouldn't let you pay?" Jill interrupted. "What gives you the right to decide?"

Dwayne cleared his throat again. Around her, Jill felt the shoulders of other students stiffen.

"I just do decide, that's all," said the boy at the back.

"You just pick dates who are scared of you," said Jill.

"Now, now. Let's not get personal," Ms. Thiessen murmured uneasily.

"It's kind of a personal subject," said Jill.

There was a pause. Then someone else spoke. Jill was surprised. This student had not said a word all semester. She usually sat in the same sweatshirt and jeans, staring out the window for the entire class. Her voice was low and absolutely even.

"I was raped once," she said. "Last summer."

Everyone was staring. Quickly, Jill looked at Ms. Thiessen. She was staring, too. The girl continued, still looking out of the window.

"Now I have a gun," she said. "I got a license for it, and I carry it all the time."

"What for?" stammered the boy at the back of the room. "That's great! Some guy comes up to you, maybe to ask you the time. And, *bang*, you shoot him?"

"No," said the girl. "Before he could get at me, I'd shoot myself."

The silence was heavy. Jill could not breathe. The girl continued to stare out the window. Ms. Thiessen dismissed the class early, asking the girl to wait behind.

As Jill left the room, vague tears stung her eyelids. Her brain seemed to have moved out of reach—for once no thought, no conclusions within her grasp.

AFTER SOCIAL HISTORY, Jill headed for Mr. Fizell's classroom. On sunny afternoons like today, the third-floor row of windows turned the chess room into a warm well-lit world of its own. Once a game started, the room would fade out around her like a clear marble, devoid of color and sound.

Sometimes, Jill concentrated so hard on a game that even her own body seemed to disappear along with the rest of the room. Today, this was what she wanted, but as she hunched over her first game, Jill found her body refused to be forgotten, would not go away. Today, it sat around her like a bruise. Quickly, she lost a game to Bertram, a boy prolific with his queen but little else. On a nearby desk, Cal sat picking at a hangnail. As Bertram moved on to another game, Cal began setting up the board.

"Today, I could take off both my rooks and my queen, and still beat you," he said.

"Yeah," muttered Jill. "Yeah, I guess." Her thoughts trailed off.

That picture was in her head—the girl from class, looking out the window in her dirty blue sweatshirt. Between her wings of uncombed hair, the pale thin lines of mouth kept moving, forming the same words. "Before he could get to me . . . Before he could get to me . . . Before he could get to me . . ."

"D' you want to play?" asked Cal.

"There was this girl in my social history class," began Jill. "She told us she got raped."

Cal reached over and began setting up her side of the board.

"I never met anyone who was raped before," said Jill.

"D' you know her?" asked Cal.

"No," said Jill. "I can't remember her name. I," she stammered, "I don't get it."

"Get what?"

"I don't get how that stuff happens," she said.

"Who does?" shrugged Cal.

"There's got to be a reason," said Jill. Her stomach shoved around inside her. "It can't just . . . happen." Cal moved out a knight. Dully, Jill stared at it. "D' you ever think about it?" she asked. "D' you ever . . . think about it?"

Cal looked directly at her. "What d' you expect from me, Jill?" he asked.

His voice was cold, his eyes a hard clear green. For a moment, she stared at him. Calmly, he looked back without blinking, waiting for her first move.

But what about the girl who got raped? Jill wanted to shout at him. You can't just go on playing chess like everything is still the way it always was.

All Cal did, finally, was blink.

Jill felt the words drag their meaning out of her throat. "From you? Nothing much." She slid out of her seat and walked quickly to the door.

"Hey, Jill."

She turned. Cal stood beside the desk, fiddling with the white king. "I thought you wanted to have a game?" His face, careful and watchful as always, was slightly flushed.

She hesitated. "Actually, I wanted to have a conversation, thanks." As she left the room, her left shoulder bumped the doorframe. She felt anger, its quick protection. She had gone to the chess room in search of Cal. He was so smart. He should have been able to explain the whole damn thing to her, tell her why it happened to that girl, to any girl.

"Incorrect assumption, m' dear," Jill muttered, pushing the outside door open. The wind was brisk, and she kicked her way through the leaves, hugging herself tightly. "IQ and compassion don't necessarily hang out together." She kicked harder at the leaves, watching them lift up and whirl away.

That had always been her assumption—smart people cared. Smart people wanted to discuss things, talk about issues. What else was a brain for?

She wandered home.

EVENING CAME. The smell of cauliflower and roast beef took over the house. Just before supper, Jill passed Dwayne on the stairs. She avoided looking at him. She could not figure out what she was feeling, and she thought that if he saw her eyes, he would know before she did. He would wring her out like a dishcloth.

"Jill?"

He stood one step lower and leaned against the wall so that their heights almost matched. He was wearing his reading glasses. Sharply defined behind the glasses, his eyes were red. "What d' you think of this afternoon?" he asked.

He's been crying, thought Jill. "Social history?" she asked.

Dwayne stared at the landing window. "I didn't know," he said softly. "All along . . . I just thought, I guess . . . it was sort of sex. Just sort of sex. I didn't know it could make anyone feel that lousy. Shit, how could she feel that lousy?"

From downstairs came the squeak of the oven door opening, then closing.

"I don't get how those things happen," said Jill.

Dwayne looked straight at her. A slight alarm gripped Jill, and she stiffened. "Are you scared of that happening?" he asked. "Y' know, to you?"

"I dunno," said Jill, looking away. The question seemed enormous. "I guess, every girl is."

"Yeah," persisted Dwayne. "But d' you think about it? Worry about it?"

Why did he want to know this? Why was he so nice all of a sudden? "I guess, sometimes."

He stared out the window again. "I'm sorry, Jill, about that football thing in the hall. I'm really sorry." He looked at her. Jill stared back. "I mean it," he added, his breath snagging on the words.

"Okay," said Jill.

There was a pause. "Well, see you at supper." Dwayne patted her clumsily on the shoulder. Then he turned and went downstairs.

Jill watched him out of sight. Then she sat and stared at the place he had been until her mother called her for supper.

THE NEXT DAY, as Jill walked through the cafeteria, she heard her name called. She turned to see Dwayne jump up from a group of boys and wave. She regarded him suspiciously as he came over, but there was such warmth in his eyes, she felt unexpectedly shy. She looked at her feet.

70

"Hey," said Dwayne. "Can you help me with something? It's with Liza."

"Liza?" Jill realized he must mean the girl from social history. "What about her?"

"Well, uh, I just want to talk to her," said Dwayne. "But I think she's afraid of guys. I was wondering if you'd come with me."

"What d' you want to talk to her about?"

"Well, just about anything. I just thought, maybe . . . maybe . . . I could make it, kind of better, y' know?"

Jill clamped down on her mouth to keep it closed. She was finding it difficult to accept that her brother was possibly functionally humane, that his brain was not a small pellet. Assumption Warp here, she thought. "Sure, Dwayne, I'll come," she said. "Where is she?"

"She's eating lunch on the stairs near the French section."

"You don't take French," said Jill. "How d' you know that? Did you go looking for her?"

"Uh, yeah." Dwayne flushed slowly. "C'mon."

Jill stared very hard at the back of his head as she followed him out of the cafeteria. Weird, she thought.

Liza was sitting hunched against the wall, staring at an unopened brown bag lunch. She wore the same blue sweatshirt. So thin, thought Jill.

"Hi," said Dwayne.

Liza looked at them quickly, then back down at her lunch. She pushed in closer to the wall, as if to let them pass. There was plenty of room. Dwayne sat down on the step below her, awkward, not knowing what to do with his good intentions. Jill sat on the stair below him. Liza's hands began to worry the opening of the lunch bag, tearing it to small pieces.

"Please go away."

Dwayne looked as if he was trying to find words the shape of his feelings and was failing miserably. Liza's hands tore at the bag. "I don't want to hurt you," said Dwayne. "I just want to talk to you."

"That's what he said," said Liza. "And then . . . "

Jill opened her mouth and threw out whatever came along. "Well, y' see, that's why I'm here," she said brightly. "Dwayne asked me to come along so then, maybe, you wouldn't feel so nervous. So that's why I'm here. Not that I don't want to be here. I sure want to be here because, well, I dunno . . . I thought maybe you needed some friends, too. It was Dwayne's idea. He wanted to help."

Jill wished she could vacuum up every word she had just spoken. But Liza was looking at them now instead of at her brown paper bag. Dwayne spoke again. It was a different voice than Jill was used to hearing—soft, with small waves.

"Did Ms. Thiessen talk to you last night?"

"She took away my gun," said Liza. "And phoned my mom. She said I was underage and couldn't have it."

"I thought you had a license for it," Jill said.

"I lied," admitted Liza. "I wish I hadn't said anything about it. Now I don't have any protection."

"There's hardly any rapists in the world," Jill started to say. Dwayne cut her off.

"Well, how 'bout us?" he asked quickly. "We'll be your protection."

"What d' you mean?" asked Liza. She gave him a nervous sidelong glance. So did Jill.

"Well, we'll walk you wherever you want to go. Like, if you want, we can walk you from class to class. And we can walk you home or if you go out in the evening. D' you go to a club or something? I'll walk you. And . . . and if you don't trust me very much, well maybe Jill could come along."

Liza frowned.

"Sure—I'll help," said Jill. She had never seen her brother so earnestly want anything. She felt she would die to help him at this moment. "We're real awesome protection," she went on. "Majorly awesome. And my schedule is totally free for you."

Dwayne grinned. "Me, too. Just the basketball team these days. Well, you've got your newspaper meetings, don't you, Jill? And chess."

"I can work around it. So, what d' you think, Liza?"

Liza hesitated.

"I really don't mind if you want Jill along," said Dwayne. "I can understand that. It won't hurt my feelings."

"Okay," said Liza slowly. She gave a greyish smile.

"First," said Dwayne, "we have to get your schedule so we can work these things out. Got a pen, Jill?"

AFTER LUNCH, Jill and Dwayne walked Liza to her class. At the midafternoon break, only the girls met because Dwayne was on the other side of the school, but he was there, grinning at the end of the day. Liza told them she lived about five blocks west of the school, then walked with her head down, saying little. It was Dwayne who began to fill the awkward space, offering to carry Liza's books, telling stories.

"You remember Skitters, Jill? Remember the time he and I went camping in grade seven? We took the pup tent and two sleeping bags and a six-pack Mom and Dad didn't know about. We biked out, parked in some farmer's field and drank the beer as fast as we could. It wasn't the first time I'd had it, but I still thought it tasted like Listerine. I think I wanted to get it out of my mouth as quick as possible. Probably Skitters was doing the same thing. God, were we pissed."

Dwayne began picking up small stones and firing them at trees. The first few times, Jill noted, Liza flinched.

"We decided," Dwayne continued, "on this competition. The idea was to get out into the middle of the road, whip down the ol' pants and leave a good dump on the yellow line, then hustle the ol' buns off to the side of the road. Then you stood and watched your offering get flattened. *Zoom! Splat!*" Dwayne started to laugh. "Skitters found out, once he got out there, he was constipated. Couldn't get it out. A car comin' round the bend caught him with his pants down, workin' away. Driver must've wondered how the moon got so low."

Jill, wondering how Liza was handling the story, felt a wash of relief as she saw the girl give a half smile. Suddenly,

Liza turned up a walkway. She lived in a duplex. She didn't ask them in but stood, shifting her feet and glancing away. Then, without a word, she turned and walked toward the porch.

"What time should we pick you up tomorrow?" Dwayne called after her.

Liza turned on the porch steps, looking startled, as if she had forgotten. "Quarter after eight." They had to strain to hear her.

"Okay," Dwayne called cheerfully. "See you tomorrow." The door closed.

Now that Liza was gone, conversation became difficult, seemed to twist out of their grasp. She wished Dwayne would come up with another story. Anything. Silent, he walked along next to her, kicking at stones. Why do I want to get to know you so much? she wondered. Why do I care?

"Dwayne," she said finally, "why are you doing this?"

It was as if she had pointed a gun at him instead of a question. He shoved his fists further inside his pockets. His eyes shut themselves in. "Why are you?" he replied.

"I was just asking a question." Suddenly, Jill's words felt raw. "If Liza asked you that question, you'd answer. You're just using me to help her. You don't care about me." Quickly, she walked away from his silence. Then she heard feet behind her, running.

"No, wait," he said, his heavy breath separating the words.

"It's not like you do this sort of thing on a daily basis," said Jill, glaring.

"You mean I don't normally do nice things?" Dwayne demanded. He cleared his throat and spat on the sidewalk.

"Oh, gross. Don't hork," complained Jill. "See—that's another thing you wouldn't do if Liza were here."

"You can take it." Dwayne glanced around in search of a distraction. "Wanna walk the tracks?"

As they crossed Edinburgh Road and headed for the railroad tracks, Jill debated the pros and cons of forgiveness. Dwayne cleared his throat again. Don't hork, she warned him silently. He swallowed. This iota of sensitivity cheered her immensely.

"I tried to talk to Cal Harding," said Jill.

"Monster Brain?" said Dwayne.

Jill laughed. "That's what you call him?"

"He's in my physics class. Thinks at the speed of light. He's all right."

"He wouldn't even talk about it. About Liza."

"Maybe he just got embarrassed talking to you about it. Didn't know what to say."

Jill reassessed her memory. Had Cal been embarrassed? Uneasy, defensive, yes. Embarrassed? Was it possible?

They reached the tracks, simultaneously stepped over the closest rail and began the walk toward home.

"Remember when we used to leave pennies on these tracks?" asked Dwayne. "We thought we could derail the whole train? Spent half my bubble gum money on it." He balanced on a rail. "A penny for a train wreck. Always wondered if I'd get stuck in jail if it happened. Wondered if they had black-and-white striped uniforms for kids." He looked down at his feet, concentrating on walking rung to rung. "I don't think I'm a super nice guy, Jill. I don't know why I do anything I do."

"Well, I don't know if I should say this." Jill watched Dwayne tense. "It's just those stories you were telling to Liza?"

"Yeah?"

"Well, they're okay most of the time, with most people, but I think they make Liza nervous."

Dwayne looked away quickly, frowning.

"It's just the stories about drinking and defecation," she explained hastily. "They're real funny, but . . . "

"No, I get what you mean. Keep the shit for another time and place," Dwayne said. He punched her shoulder lightly. "Like you said, I don't do this sort of thing on a daily basis. Anytime I sound like an idiot, just let me know."

The tracks curved ahead of them. As early evening descended, houses and trees darkened. Cars were beginning to turn on their headlights. Peace began to settle over Jill, soak through her entire body. Dwayne bent down, picked up a small stone and placed it carefully on one of the steel rails. "For the next train," he grinned.

JILL DIALED Deb's number. "Deb, I have a survey question for you."

"Where've you been the last coupla days?" complained Deb. "I had to eat lunch by myself, in the cafeteria."

Alone in the bologna sandwich jungle, thought Jill. "Sorry. Busy. Hey, I need your opinion."

"What for?" Already Deb's confidence had gone into a state of shock.

"D' you think the legs competition is sexist?"

"Won't you get into trouble for asking that?" asked Deb.

"I'm just asking a question," Jill protested.

"Sexist?" repeated Deb. "I dunno. That's such a tough question, Jill."

Cheez Whiz, thought Jill. Deb was like Cheez Whiz. Squeeze a nonopinion out of her, it was always the same pasty content. "Well, d' you think the Miss America Pageant is sexist?" demanded Jill.

"Oh, I dunno," said Deb. "Geez, Jill." There was a long pause. Jill let it plod on. She would not allow her friend to escape the responsibility of thought. "Well, they get money and prizes for it, don't they?"

"But is it sexist?" asked Jill. "I know it's legal."

Deb did not like pauses. She filled this one with small between-word sounds. "No," she said, at length. "No, it's not sexist."

"Okay, Deb," sighed Jill. "Thanks."

"You don't like my answer," worried Deb.

"I'll promise to forget it was yours," said Jill.

JILL STARED at the picture of the erect penis in her health textbook. So it got bigger. So what did that mean? How much bigger? And how big was it in the first place?

SLAVE TRADER

It'd be nice if they gave you some measurements, she reflected. So you had a little idea of what to expect. This whole idea of something getting bigger—it sounded a little alarming. What if it kept getting bigger? What if you didn't have enough room for it? Did it get bigger before or after it got inside you?

Jill closed the textbook quickly, hoping the thoughts would get caught between the pages, stay there and leave her alone. I am a Victim Of My Brain, she thought, observing her hairy legs. They were pale and knobby, full of short dark bristles, like skinny cartoon legs. Not comforting. From just below the knees, she looked like Popeye the Sailorman in shorts.

THE SOCIAL HISTORY CLASS had established its seating plan in early September. The boys club sprawled against the back window. The middle desks emanated mediocrity. The front ones boasted the highest quota of zits per capita. Jill had settled for mediocrity. Dwayne anchored the class at the back. At the left front corner, around Liza, was a half circle of empty desks.

The following class, Dwayne walked in with Liza. Jill paused behind them, unsure. It occurred to her, suddenly, that she wasn't sure if challenging a seating plan was a constitutional right. Without comment, without hesitation, Dwayne walked over to the window and sat down in front of Liza.

Jill's eyes bulged. Don't be such a beagle, she told herself. Makes sense. She sat down next to Liza.

"D' you mind if I sit here?" she asked.

Liza hesitated, then shook her head. Ms. Thiessen, noting the change of position, smiled but did not comment. Jill could not help but be aware of the stares of other students. None of their classmates had ever seen Jill or Dwayne acknowledge a shared family tree. As they migrated to the back corner, a few boys joked with Dwayne. He grinned and nodded but stayed in place, turning halfway

77

around in his seat. Every now and then, he made a comment to Liza.

Jill watched her brother. She felt him pick his words as if
each one had to be exactly right. Quick learner, she thought.
Not once did he force Liza's eyes. His own gaze flicked over
Ms. Thiessen, the blackboard, other students, winked at Jill,
flicked back to his own feet, his hands. At most, it would
touch Liza's desk, her fingertips.

How did he know not to sit behind her? Jill wondered.
How did he know Liza would want to be able to see him?

Once the class commenced, Jill watched Liza begin to
observe Dwayne. She began the class by staring at her desk.
Then, in quick glances, she examined the bottom stripe of
Dwayne's rugby shirt. Then, it was the second stripe from
the bottom. She progressed, stripe by stripe, up his back,
examining his collar, his neck, his hair. Though she could see
his profile, Liza avoided the face.

After this, Liza stared down again, digging a thumbnail
into the back of her other hand.

ALL THIS STUFF about movement, Jill reflected, and
change . . . . She stared at the CD cover, watching the waterfall. The music twisted constantly inside her, sometimes gently, sometimes painfully. She could see the characters moving
about in the jungle—the Jesuit, the slave trader, the Guaraní.
His Eminence. The priest had God's face. His Eminence had
the devil's face. Their expressions didn't change much. But
then there was the slave trader's face. He started off as the
bad guy, killing his brother and trading slaves and all that.
But once the priest took him back up the river, he became a
good guy.

There's a scene, Jill thought, where his face changes like
the waterfall. It's when the Guaraní forgive him for what he's
done to their people. He's been dragging a bundle of
weapons and armor up the side of the waterfall as penance
for killing his brother. The Guaraní take the bundle off his
back and throw it away.

The slave trader cries and cries. Then, it's as if his face slides from crying into laughter, as if the edges flow together and his guilt and all the bad stuff washes away.

On the other side of her head sat His Eminence, his face like a stone carving. All the singing of the Guaraní, their beautiful voices, did not seem to get to him at all. Guess he didn't feel like he needed their forgiveness, Jill decided. "What d' you expect from me, Jill?" his eyes asked. "What d' you expect from yourself?"

The CD ended. Jill found herself back in her own body again, heavy. She looked at her hand, and it seemed strange, deformed. Frowning, she wondered if Liza ever felt like her body was the wrong place to be. So many times, Jill reflected, it'd be nice just to live inside your head and never come out.

"JUST TRY TO FIND a teenage brain north of the U.S. border with any Canadian content," scoffed Cal. "Try."

"I'm proud of being Canadian," protested Jill. She moved a pawn, sat back and observed the board. Rats. She'd just destroyed the complete vertebrae of her defense. Cal was quick to move in for the kill.

"I listen to the CBC," continued Jill, trying to ignore her rapidly inflating expectation of defeat. "And I can list all the competitors in the last Liberal leadership race. I know all the premieres, even the ones in the Territories."

"What's your favorite movie?" Cal tested.

"The Mission. Takes place in South America."

"Not bad, but it's made by Americans." He took her queen. "Checkmate."

Jill stared at the board. This was her first visit to the chess room in a while. Liza had left school early for an appointment. "I'm taking a survey," she said. "Will you answer the question?"

"I would feel honored," said Cal.

"It's not that big a deal." Although Dwayne's explanation had convinced Jill she might have been wrong about Cal's reaction, she had decided to maintain an emotional distance of at least twenty kilometers at all times. "Do you think the legs competition is sexist?" She tried not to look expectant. How would this individual sidestep the issue?

"Yes," said Cal. "Isn't that obvious?"

Jill wrote down, "Yes, isn't that obvious?" next to *Cal*. She felt him graph the unexpected lack of curve in her response factor.

"*Telegraph* survey?" he asked.

"Nope. Mine. Thanks for the game, Cal."

"Yeah," he said. "Sure."

She turned at the door, smiling at the careful quiet stillness of his face. "Try eating an American flag," she called. "I hear it makes you shit stars."

He grinned.

THOUGH IT HAD BEEN Dwayne's idea, it was Jill who ended up spending the most time with Liza. He was there every morning, but basketball practices and games scooped up most of his afternoons. Jill did not really mind. She was tired of the skid marks everyone seemed to be leaving on her emotions. Liza was concave, where everyone else was convex. She left Jill's brain alone. At least she made no aggressive claims on it. But a sort of blur was always around her, the presence of some unworded pain. It worried Jill.

What if she said the wrong thing, some dumb series of words? It wasn't as if she'd never done it before. Every time Jill showed up at Liza's locker or front door, a billboard flashed across her brain: WHAT DO YOU SAY TO SOMEBODY WHO GOT RAPED? I mean, thought Jill, you can't just talk about the price of Oscar Meyer wieners. Her mind reeled at this verbal betrayal. Wieners! God. See? I can't talk to a rape victim. Here I am wanting to talk about wieners.

When Dwayne was there, Jill let him do the talking. Since her microscopic coaching session with him, no words like *wieners* ever got out of his mouth. Around Liza, inappropriate language temporarily erased itself from his vocabulary.

ARLENE WAS BACK in science class. Whatever had caused her temporary absence had not been Death. Disappointed, Jill sidled around Lyle and Chuck, who had glued themselves to Arlene's half of their desk, sat down, opened her Duotang and began to conjugate.

"Hey, Jill." Suddenly, a hand spread out over *puer in atrium est*—a boy's hand. It was Peter.

Please be normal, she hissed at her hormones. "Hi, Peter."

Suddenly, there was silence. She checked. Yes, her peripheral vision was functional. Arlene and the boys were watching. Arlene snickered.

"Hey, I got another survey question," Jill said.

"Great."

Words, conversation. They functioned like two blind rabbits under the hovering hawks next door.

"So, what is it?" Peter's ears grew redder by the millisecond.

"Do you think the legs competition is sexist?" Jill felt alarm flap about in her head like laundry on a backyard line. Oh, oh. She had meant to give the question about the cafeteria menu.

The bell rang. Without reply, Peter moved on. He must hate her for asking him that question, especially in front of the death squad. I thought you didn't care about Arlene, Jill yelled at Peter in her head. I thought you meant the three point five.

"Put me down as a judge for the competition," said Lyle. "We're all a *No* for your survey."

Jill did not want to acknowledge Lyle's presence by looking at him, but found her face turning in his direction.

"Put us all down for a *No*," he repeated.

For a brief moment, Arlene's eyes lost their focused contempt. "I suppose that's all right with me," she drawled.

"Sure," said Jill. "Three *No*'s."

Chuck did not comment. He watched her write it down.

"I SHOULDN'T HAVE SAID that in class."

The words came, sudden, unexpected, from Liza's mouth.

"Said what?" asked Jill. She wished Dwayne was there.

The two girls shared Jill's black umbrella, though half of Liza soaked up rain. She doesn't want to touch me, thought Jill.

"About the gun. About . . . "

. . . the rape, Jill finished silently. She did not want to talk about it.

"Everybody knows," said Liza.

"Things do get around."

"They look at you different," said Liza.

"What d' you mean?" Guilt was taking up a lot of space.

Liza's voice sounded thin, high, as if it could snap and be gone anytime. "They look at you like you're dirty." She made a small gasp. "Like, like you wanted it."

"Who does?"

Liza looked up between the umbrella's dripping points. She spoke with her teeth clenched, filtering the words. "Coupla guys asked me to do it with them."

"I'd like to stick their faces in a blender," said Jill.

Liza continued in the same tone, as if Jill had not spoken. "I didn't really tell the truth about all of it."

Jill breathed quickly. Enough already.

"There was no guy in an alley," said Liza. A moan pulled itself from her mouth. "It was my brother."

The air was suddenly gone. Jill could not get any of it into her. Liza cried, her words ripped apart, coming in fragments.

"Older. Not around a lot. He came home. Summer. I was . . . afraid . . . of him. I tried . . . to keep away. He said . . . things. Looked at me. Mom works . . . at a diner."

"Where was your dad?" asked Jill.

"Divorced." Liza's face twisted. "One night, he kept saying . . . things. Drank a bunch of beer. He grabbed me. Wouldn't let me . . . " Suddenly Liza doubled over and groaned. The sound clawed at Jill. What do I do? she thought, staring at her friend's bent form. Friend—this was her friend, now.

Liza sank to the grass and rolled into a small ball. She kept groaning, dragging air in between the sounds. Jill's stomach sagged. Confusion hemorrhaged in her. "Liza? Liza?" she kept saying, patting her shoulder. Then Jill dropped the umbrella and sat down beside the girl. The rain poured wet hair into her eyes. When would Liza stop and get up?

After a while, Jill tried to pull Liza up and managed to get her leaned against her shoulder. The cold water clogged her eyelashes, stung her eyes. Her clothes clung to her like wet palms. Inch by inch, cold traveled into her body, leaving only the thin hot line that folded her stomach in half.

The whole time, traffic kept driving by. A few people passed, sloppy in the rain. What to say? Words felt like soggy paper on her tongue. Liza did not hold onto Jill, but she did not move away from her shoulder either. After a while, the deep moans subsided. A while after that, the smaller cries stopped. Then there was just the regular swish of rush-hour traffic, the mind-numbing rain.

When Jill tried to pick up her umbrella, her joints cracked. It was difficult to move. "Let's go, okay?" she said.

Jill let the umbrella drag along the cement. They walked along, silent. At the duplex, Liza stopped on the first step, then turned. She looked at Jill's collar, hesitated and met her eyes.

"Can your brother come here?" Jill asked.

"He can't come to the house," said Liza. "There's something called a restraining order from the police."

"D' you want to come to our house for supper?" asked Jill.

"No." Liza walked to her front door and opened the screen. Jill thought she might turn, say something, but after a pause, Liza unlocked the front door and walked in. The door closed again.

Jill stood without moving in the sound of all that rain. It fell onto every inch of an already wet world. The first drop, she thought, started without anybody noticing, just like the first hurt that had happened long ago to this world. Probably, the first drop fell nowhere, evaporated before it even hit the planet. And the first pain went away fast. But the rest followed and kept falling and falling. How come things just kept getting sadder and sadder?

Jill walked the tracks for a while, bumping the umbrella point rung to rung. The rails glistened on and on until they took the curve ahead of her and slid on toward a time and place that were out of sight.

JILL DID NOT TELL DWAYNE about Liza's brother. The truth told in that afternoon of cold rain shrank down to a small grey square, like a photograph. Jill filed it somewhere deep inside herself, so far in that she hoped she could forget about it. But the memory sat there in the middle of everything she said and did, in the middle of herself, something alien.

The rest of her life and time kept going on and on, swirling around her. But the small grey square stayed where she had put it, a very little window with the shade pulled down.

Dwayne was too cheerful, too hopeful about things. He had a generic sort of hope, Jill decided, because he did not know the details. Maybe that was good. Maybe it was better not to know too much.

THEY WERE STANDING, rows of girls in blue, stretched out across the gym floor. Supposedly, they were doing a shoulder-pass drill in parallel lines of six. Back and forth, the ball traveled, snapped out from the wrists. The girls had been told to find the most direct line between two points.

Jill's goose bumps were on the prowl. They made her leg hairs stand up straighter. She hated this. She stood, dreading the moment of contact with the ball. It tore through the fluorescent lighting, her thoughts and thudded into her, knocking the air from her chest, slamming her hands against her chin.

Abominable Karen stood opposite her. Jill was sweating. Her blood was subzero, but still she sweated. Survival mode on a long-term basis must confuse the immune system. Jill flip-flopped between options. If she watched Karen's eyes, she could not see where the ball was coming from or which part of her body would probably be removed upon contact. If she watched the ball, she could not evaluate Karen's mood, the viciousness of its trajectory. The ball's surface of fine edges was there again, a thick sudden reality cutting slightly into her palms. After she shoved it into the air toward the next girl, Jill's palms pulsed with heat.

Ever since she had seen those first minuscule filaments of unshaved hair on Jill's legs, Karen had decided to notice Jill—everything she did, everything she said. Everything I don't do, everything I neglect to say, Jill sighed to herself.

What was it about fluorescent lighting that sucked the humor out of you? Probably in twenty years, scientists would discover it caused cancer or sterility. Or brain damage. When you were around it, you didn't think. All you did was react, do what you were told. Perfect for gym class.

The ball hit her between the eyes, a very direct connection between two points. Jill's head bounced back, her feet stumbling to keep up. She could not hear the laughter, but she felt it dance around her. She bent over, gripping her head.

Ms. Cottrell stepped through the air into three dimensions and bent over her. "Let me see," her voice said. Jill opened her eyes. The coach filled them entirely.

"It's just a headache," Jill said.

"You'll be all right," Ms. Cottrell boomed. "Sit this one out on the bench."

The bench was heaven. Jill practiced the look of a headache victim, squinting at the clock behind its wire mask.

There were twenty minutes to go, blurred around the edges. Look ill, she told herself. Look very ill. Dead, even.

THE HALLOWEEN DANCE loomed, social bookmark that it was. Jill hated school dances. It was not the actual dancing itself that she hated. It was the pressure of dancing in front of everyone else and trying to get it right.

Jill wanted to go to this dance with Peter, but she figured she had blown it with that brain-dead question about the legs competition being sexist. Should she take a chance and ask him anyway? She thought about this as she skipped down the stairs from the languages section *en route* to photocopy a form for Mr. Sinclair. The halls were empty of all but afternoon sunlight.

But dancing in front of other kids made her feel like such a dolt. She had attended her junior high grad dance and another dance three months into high school. Each time, her body had betrayed her. If she was sitting still listening to music, she felt the music inside her, taking beautiful fragile shapes. But at dances, between other kids who were all enthusiastically swinging their elbows, knees, hips, her body turned to wood.

Jill turned down a hall toward the office. Then she saw Peter up ahead at his locker. Her feet slowed and stopped. She wanted to ask him so much. How did she get past that question from science class?

As she stood there pondering the possibilities, Jill saw Peter look up toward her. Suddenly, she could not face him. It was as if someone took hold of her face, turned it away and made her look at a nearby garbage pail. A garbage pail! Jill pulled her eyes away. She did not want to be seen standing there and observing a garbage pail as if her life depended upon it. She wanted to walk up to Peter and ask him to go to the dance.

But she could not. She just could not. Still, to get to the office, she had to walk by him. As she approached his general direction, Jill's heart began a body slam. Her eyes made a minute examination of the large concrete blocks in the wall. When she thought she must have reached his locker, she looked up, trying to be casual. No one was there.

She was sure Peter had seen her. Briefly, she reached out and touched his locker. Down the hall, a class door suddenly opened. Jill turned and walked quickly to the office.

DURING THE NIGHT, the first snow fell, then more during the afternoon. In Exhibition Park, muddy footprints tracked the white surface. The wind brushed their ears a cold red.

Dwayne swung himself up the steps of the playground slide, seating himself at the top. Outlined against the bare trees, he hunched down into his jacket collar. Liza leaned against the slide's steps and watched.

Jill hooked her arms around the slide's supporting pole because it was too cold to hang onto with her hands. As she swung herself around it, the park became a series of overlapping circles. Jill let Liza and Dwayne talk without her. Round and round—the trees, the sky, the slide, the trees, the sky . . . . They blurred together like mixed-up faces—the priest, the slave trader, His Eminence, the priest, the slave trader, His Eminence . . . .

She stopped. There was the slight smell of smoke. Stumbling, Jill pushed herself away from the pole. Dwayne and Liza were three Dwaynes, three Lizas. They gradually reorganized into one of each. They were both smoking.

Since when had Dwayne been smoking? The park spread out in browns, greys and blacks from the figures of Dwayne and Liza. The cigarettes in their hands made the scene suddenly unfamiliar, like an unknown picture she had come across.

"I didn't know you smoked."

Dwayne did not answer. His eyes studied her face. This is a test, Jill thought. You want to pass. Watch the Mouth Warp.

In the corner of Jill's eye, Liza shifted, an uneasy movement. "Sometimes I smoke," she offered. "Sometimes you need it."

"Well, no—it's not that." Jill tried to defend her tone. "I guess I just didn't know. One of life's little surprises." She concentrated on making a fan of muddy brown footprints in the snow. Her runners were beginning to feel wet. Why did Dwayne do this? It made her feel lonely, shut out of his mood changes like this, when he went off somewhere, off into some other reality and would not take her with him.

"Haven't you tried it?" asked Liza.

"Yeah," said Jill. "Last year. I felt like a furnace."

Dwayne snorted. "You can wheeze like an accordion."

"When did you start?" she asked him.

Dwayne pondered. "Grade five? Someone had a pack—y' know how it goes." He shrugged.

"No," said Jill, "I guess I don't."

"I guess that's why I didn't tell you," said Dwayne. "But like you said, no big deal. Want one?"

Jill hesitated. She could look cool, like the Marlboro Man. "No, not really."

He dropped the cigarette butt and watched it burn in the snow. Liza tapped a long line of ash. Smokers always had something to do with their hands. Jill shoved hers into her pockets.

"It's almost Halloween," Liza said. "You two going to the dance tomorrow?"

"Yeah," said Dwayne. "You, Jill?"

Jill stared at her soggy runners. Maybe Peter had not seen her in the hall. She could still ask him, couldn't she? Sure. Could he have missed her?

Not a chance. "No, I don't think so," she replied.

"Me neither." Liza gave an uncertain smile. "Too many people."

JILL WATCHED Liza's face as the three of them sat eating lunch on the back stairwell. Dwayne was elaborating on Baseball Story Number Seven. Jill knew them all. They had been impaled through repetition into her brain.

"This kid, Steve—he's petrified of overrunning second or third base. Someone told him he could only overrun first, see? So he hits the ball and takes off for first base. He passes first, and he keeps going—runs past first, through the infield, through the outfield, and we lose sight of him. He keeps running until he's out on the street."

Dwayne relived stories as he told them. Right now, Jill figured, he was somewhere on Exhibition Street, dodging Toyotas and Fords.

Sometimes, it was as if Liza's face actually shifted on the bone. The tight wary expression unclenched and let go for a bit, but then it seemed as if she did not know what to do with her expression so only little things happened, like flickers of smiles or a quick pink touch on her cheek. Jill wanted to see Liza's face slide into a joy as sudden and complete as the slave trader's had done in the movie. It would be such a wonderful moment. Liza would be happy and healed and finished with the gross horrible problem sticking to her guts.

Dwayne was back at home plate, warming up for Baseball Story Number Eight. Jill watched Liza's face and tried to figure out an action plan for demolishing bad memories, the rotten lousy things life stuck some people with.

NATIVES

Coach Booth attended the early November Telegraph meeting, filling his rugby shirt with muscles and good humor. "Ah, Dwayne Gilbert's little sister."

"I think so," said Jill. She sat down.

Coach laughed loudly. He spread out on each side of the student-sized desk like a child's picture colored beyond the lines. His conversation, his moods—everything about Coach was like that, bigger and louder than it needed to be.

Ewald sighed. He had deserted phys. ed. as soon as it was possible. In grade ten, phys. ed. was mandatory. In grade eleven, it was not. Just like that, the system decided students knew enough about muscles and blood cells to perform basic physical movements without instruction. "Mr. Booth, was there anything particular you wanted to talk about today?"

"No, no, no. I'm just here to see how it's all coming along," said Coach. "Here I am, the staff supervisor. Thought I should show up once in a while. Not that I don't think it's in very capable hands, of course." He repeated his laugh.

It was one of those meetings where Ewald had collected them all to ensure they were doing their correct little performances in print. Jill wished she had skipped the meeting. It was the first time Dwayne had walked Liza home without her. The thought made her uneasy somehow.

"How's the survey coming along, Jill?"

Jill focused on Ewald. Survey. The cafeteria question. "I haven't started."

"Are you going to be finished for the deadline?" asked Ewald. "Next Wednesday?"

She was tripping him up in front of Coach. "I'm not sure."

"Jill, are you sure you're interested in doing the surveys?" Ewald said.

Now she faltered. Nice work. Making her decide in front of Coach. "I'll get it done," she muttered.

Coach Booth rumbled about a bit inside his rugby shirt. "How are the entries for the legs competition coming along?"

"We have ten," said Ewald.

"Needs a bit of a promo," observed Coach. "How 'bout some new posters? Some PA announcements?"

"The office told us we couldn't use the PA," Ewald told him. "It's because it's just part of the Christmas Carousel Assembly. Posters should be okay."

"Oh," said Coach. He seemed to be dribbling his thoughts around, assessing the distance for an off-the-boards shot. He aimed, fired, made it through. "Maybe I can talk to the principal. See what I can do," he said importantly.

"Um," suggested Jill. Something moved inside her head, making her a little dizzy. She frowned and blinked.

"Excuse me, Jill?" Ewald sounded alarmed. His fingers were fiendishly at work with his top button. "Is this something we've already discussed? As a team? Something we've already come to a majority decision on?"

It was an image from the movie—His Eminence. He was sitting in the middle of her head. Jill tried to ignore him. "Mr. Booth," she continued, "d' you think the legs competition is sexist?"

Ewald sighed and made progress with his buttons. His

Eminence nodded slowly, approvingly. The question had come out like a correct shoulder pass, snapped from the wrists. Shortest path between two points.

Coach's chin jerked slightly back. "No, no," he said. Then, "No, no, no, no, no." Dribbling that thought around, Jill mused, trying to assess the hoop shot. "No, no, Jill." Now he had figured out his next sentence. "I think you're going a bit overboard. A little extreme. It's just a little fun, that's all."

"Jill is one of our competitors," Ewald mentioned.

Jill noticed Rob shift in his seat. Beth yawned. It came out as a pink bubble.

"Well, there. If you're one of the competitors, you can't have much of a problem with it," remonstrated Coach.

"Well, I do," said Jill.

"Oh, brother," Renita muttered.

"Well, why did you enter then, Jill?" The words came out quicker, harsher than Coach had contemplated. His good mood narrowed.

Jill felt their eyes shove at her. She looked at His Eminence, who shrugged. How to communicate? she wondered. The thoughts were there. She wanted to get them out—out where they could be heard. It was all part of . . . all part of . . . a bigness. A larger bigness that was wrong, that was like a huge heaviness sitting on all of them. But no one seemed to even notice. No one noticed anything.

Suddenly, Jill realized why she always wore black—it stood out better in a crowd.

By the time Coach's next words slid into her brain, Jill realized that her thoughts had gotten stuck somewhere inside, like flies on flypaper. No one had heard her reasons except His Eminence.

"Y' see, Jill, when you think about it, it isn't really such a big deal, is it?" cajoled Coach. "Lighten up, kid."

Jill spun her pen around and around on her desk. Lighten up, kid. Put on a pink attitude. Wear a frill on your smile.

His Eminence sighed. Ewald lost a shirt button. It dropped onto the floor with a small sound.

JILL LAY ON HER BED. She had pulled one of her sweat pant legs up above the knee and rested that ankle against the other bent knee. She studied the pattern of hairs growing over her leg. It was an invading army. The longest mightiest hair measured over half an inch. The hairs gave her a baleful glare, then resumed growing.

Jill pondered. What was the current world record for the longest female leg hair? Did women in colder climates grow thicker hair, then weave it into carpets to sell? Maybe that's what was meant by *natural fibers*. Jill tried braiding the hairs.

The hairs swarmed over her leg in a distinct pattern. Even her toes had a few hairs. A general fluff fuzzed the top of her foot. But the real stuff began around the ankle. Where the calf muscle started, the hairs became shorter and thinner. Most of them grew up the front to just below the kneecap.

Very weird, thought Jill. Leg hair can't be for protection against the environment. What's the point? Knee socks accomplished the same purpose. They probably did a better job against cold and bruising. Why hadn't evolution and centuries of sock wearing caused the human body to eliminate leg hair?

With her pen, she drew outlines around some of the longest hairs, then gave them Mickey Mouse hats. Leg hair sure is ugly, she thought. How would she ever get used to it?

"JILL."

She turned. It was Mr. Fizell. "We haven't seen you in the chess room for quite a while," he said, studying her from above his chin–hand connection. "Something the matter?"

"Well, uh, no," said Jill. She had forgotten the chess room, its rounded quiet.

"There's a tournament this weekend," said Mr. Fizell. "We're hosting it here in the cafeteria. Ten a.m. I'd like to see you on the team."

"Oh," said Jill.

"Are you interested?" he asked.

"Sure," said Jill. "Okay."

"Good," said Mr. Fizell. "Come in and play a few games if you find the time."

"I will," said Jill. "I will."

SHE SAW HIM in her head. He sat on a canopied chair, leaning forward. On his face, His Eminence wore a silent expression.

Jill shook her head so hard that her bedroom moved in small circles, but His Eminence remained completely still at the center. He had been there for the last hour. No matter which textbook she looked at—Latin, science, health—he sat there in the middle of it. He never changed position, never said a thing.

"Look, d' you mind coming back some other time?" Jill said. "I don't want to be rude about this, but I'm busy. I've got to study—y' know, Reality Therapy. Figments of imagination have got to go home now."

His Eminence looked away, always away, toward the same spot. She felt a sigh pick up her body and put it down again. "You're getting me off track," she muttered. "I wish I knew why I keep thinking about you. I just don't see why you did what you did."

He was so still that with that wig, he could have been something out of a Baroque painting.

"What're you doing in my head?" she asked.

There was no answer.

"COME DOWNTOWN with me after class," suggested Deb.

Jill sidestepped Deb's eyes and looked out the Latin class windows. "I can't. I'm busy."

"What're you so busy with these days?"

"I've got to meet Liza and Dwayne," said Jill.

"You used to hate your brother," complained Deb. "And who's this Liza all of a sudden?"

"Didn't I mention her before?" asked Jill.

"No," said Deb. "And you're starting to talk like your brother, too. No straight answers."

Jill felt a smile line the inside of her mouth, but she kept it there. "Have you figured out whether or not the legs competition is sexist?"

"No," said Deb.

Jill felt irritation sharpen her words. "No, you haven't, or no, you don't think so?" she asked.

"Just no," said Deb.

Greg Sacuta walked in. Mr. Sinclair followed, a weak shadow. "Perhaps we could begin?" he asked.

THE LUNCH-TIME SUNLIGHT warmed the stairwell walls and linoleum. Jill shifted. Her bum was going numb.

"I want to get a Coke," said Dwayne. "Hey, why don't we go down to the cafeteria?" He leaned forward, about to stand up.

No, Jill thought. No, Dwayne. She knew that probably he hadn't felt it, the way Liza had tensed at his suggestion. Anything could happen down there in that cafeteria crowd. Anything.

"C'mon," encouraged Dwayne. He reached over and touched Liza's hand. "I'll buy you a pop." She pulled back so quickly that one shoulder thudded against the wall.

"No, Dwayne," Jill said softly. Their eyes met. You don't know what it means to be afraid like this, she thought at him. You have no idea.

Dwayne studied her eyes for a long time. No, not studied, Jill thought later. It was almost as if he was holding them gently in the palm of his hand and was turning them this way and that, trying to understand everything about them. A small confused frown chased itself across his forehead, and his eyebrows shifted. She watched the mood change in his eyes, the slight difference in color, the lines at the corners.

"Okay," he said very quietly. "Sorry. I don't really need that Coke. Sorry. About your hand."

Head bowed and silent, Liza stared at her feet. Above her,

hovering in the air like some misplaced saint, His Eminence suddenly appeared, arms crossed and nodding wisely. Jill sucked her breath in and blinked fiercely. She began to talk.

"Oh, yeah, the first tournament I played in, I was the only girl, and . . . " Use the words, any words, she thought, to stitch the air back together again so we can all breathe normally again. Please.

PETER DID NOT TALK to her anymore. When he came into science class, he made an immediate right, so close to the wall that he almost scraped off paint. He continued to skim the wall with his shoulder until he reached the desk he shared with Amil, second row from the back.

The Arlene Experiment had failed miserably, and Arlene did not even know it. Jill thought of the desk she shared with Arlene as another planet she had to land on temporarily. A girls washroom was directly across the hall from the science classroom. If she synchronized her watch, she was able to zoom across the galaxy and land on her side of Arlene's territory seconds before the bell rang.

Sometimes, if his schedule allowed it, His Eminence would join her, sitting between Arlene and herself, his eyes focused attentively on the science teacher. This was, Jill had to admit, a relief. With His Eminence between them, she could pretend that Arlene was not there, had never been there, would not be there again. Now if she could just get the legate to blot out Karen, the entire phys. ed. class and maybe Greg Sacuta while he was at it . . . .

AS JILL AND DWAYNE WALKED away from Liza's house, snow dropped into the grey world, taking the sharp edges off sound, muffling Edinburgh Road traffic. They walked opposite rails on the tracks, balancing. In the slow white fall, they were the only dark shapes moving, shoulder to shoulder, toward the Edinburgh Road crossing.

"Dwayne," said Jill, "what's sex like?"

Dwayne pulled the cigarette from his mouth, exhaled and

stopped. A lot more snow seemed to come down before he answered. "That depends on who you're with," he said. He took one last drag on the cigarette, then ground out the butt. "And on what you want, I guess."

Jill waited while he lit another cigarette.

"Y' see," he continued, "sometimes you want different things. Sometimes you feel different than other times. Sometimes, when you're drunk, you just want to let 'er rip." He paused again. "Other times . . . other times it's different. You feel like you want to put everything you've got into it. You want to make it right in a way you can't talk about."

Jill watched her right foot dig into the gravel. "Dwayne, what's an erection like?"

Dwayne inhaled and exhaled slowly. "Whoa."

Jill's eyes examined each snap of his school jacket until she could look at his face. He was grinning. "You want color scheme and measurements?"

"Radius, diameter," Jill giggled. "Is there some sort of pi r^2 formula?"

"I guess it's geometric," he admitted.

"Well, they never tell you in health class. We get these line drawings and they talk about it getting bigger and you end up wondering if it's an invasion from outer space or something. I dunno, sometimes you just wish you knew a little more about it. At least, what you're supposed to expect."

"Guys got the same problem. We just get drawings to go on, too."

"Well, it's not supposed to hurt you like hell the first time, is it?"

They started to walk on again, shoulders brushing. "It can," said Dwayne. "I've heard guys talk about that." He frowned. "It's hard to explain. You can do the same thing with the same girl at different times and feel completely different." He paused. "And erections do come in different sizes." He grinned suddenly. "It can be, oh, ten, twenty, thirty inches."

"Like this?" Jill measured the air with her hands.

"Oh, Christ, Jill," laughed Dwayne. "We're talking humans, here, not belugas."

"Well, what is ten inches, then?" demanded Jill.

"I dunno. Check it out with a ruler," said Dwayne. "Anyways, most of them come way, way shorter than that."

"Well, how 'bout . . . how thick they get?" asked Jill.

"You're really getting specific, aren't you?" muttered Dwayne. "Maybe a coupla inches . . . I dunno. Most guys talk about length, not width. It'll be all right, Jill. Don't do it when you're drunk, and do it with some guy who's hung around for a long time."

"How long's a long time?" asked Jill.

"Oh, five, ten minutes," said Dwayne. "And now," he continued, grounding out his cigarette, "I am going to shut you up by filling your mouth with snow. Hope it'll freeze your brain."

JILL STILL FOUND IT HARD to attach names to penises, bodies to penises. Bodies seemed so big, so competent . . . so reasonable. They moved from one function to the next, entirely within control, well within the realm of logic. But these penises—they were these strange, wrinkled, dangling things. What did they have to do with Dwayne, Peter, Cal, Mr. Sinclair, her dad? Santa? Did Santa have one?

And what was the relationship between the penis and Liza's brother? His Eminence sighed and shook his head.

You have one, too, Jill told him silently.

THE CATHOLIC GIRLS SCHOOL was at the next chess tournament. There were a lot more kids this time, almost double the number that had been at Jill's first one. As she shrugged off her black coat, Mr. Fizell waved at her from across the cafeteria. She saw Cal already hunched over a board. Checking the schedule, she found her name and seat. Her first opponent had a very loud cold and squeezed his concentration in between sneezes. Jill defeated him quickly. The second proved to be more difficult.

The team from Cambridge had not been listed as blind, but the girl sitting across the board certainly was. She made no reply to Jill's greeting, erasing the significance of friendly formalities. Jill had the brief sensation of her own face being wiped off.

It was a specialty board. The players were pegged into the board and notched on the top, according to position and team. The girl took a long time to place each move, running her fingers constantly across the tops of the players. When she had completed her move, she would rest her fingers on the table. They kept smoothing its surface, as if the movement recalled the bumps and notches of her position to the girl's mind.

Jill did not want to play this game. Or rather, she did not want to compete against this girl. The girl's concentration was so intense; it held on by the tips of its fingernails. Jill hated every move she made. She hated thinking toward the win she knew she would take. She hated feeling sorry for this girl who would hate her for feeling sorry for her. The girl said nothing to Jill's "Checkmate." She said nothing to Jill's "Good-bye."

Jill lost her third game. She joined the group watching Cal's final match. He and his opponent were using a sand clock. Cal was losing. She could tell by the way he was hanging onto his hair. The sand clock ran for one minute at a time. The other boy took his entire minute for each move, then turned the clock over. Immediately, Cal shoved a piece to another square, grabbed the sand clock and slammed it back over. The other boy jerked. He was beginning to sweat. Cal gave him no time. Time would have been generous. Inevitably, Cal wore him down and won another game.

"We wanted to have a prize for the girls section," Mr. Fizell told Jill. "There are nine of you this time. You came in first. Congratulations."

Nine girls and thirty-eight boys, Jill thought, teetering on the edge of a refusal. She was tired of this balancing act. "Thank-you," she said and took the twenty dollars.

"WHAT DO YOU THINK OF PAWNS, JILL?"
Jill stopped cleaning her room. She was getting used to

His Eminence hovering for hours in her brain, but he had been a silent movie up to this point.

"Excuse me?"

"What do you think of pawns?" he repeated.

"Pawns?" she asked. "You use them to protect the more important pieces."

His Eminence's face smiled. "Listen to them sometime," he said. "They have the most beautiful voices."

"What?" asked Jill. "The pawns have voices?"

His Eminence turned his face away again, back to its customary profile. Jill held her body in the same position while she tried to figure this one out. She did not let herself breathe. What had just happened in her head?

"Pardon?" she asked.

There was no answer.

"WHAT'RE YOU LOOKING AT, JILL?"

Karen sat at the T intersection of the aisle that Jill's gym locker was on. Jill stared at the other girl's sweat socks. They were snow white, probably smelled Downy fresh.

"Nothing," Jill protested.

Karen sat in her bra and panties, tapping one foot. A few of the other girls turned toward Jill.

"Sure you were. You're always staring at me," insisted Karen. "Why're you always staring at me, Jill?"

All of Jill's thoughts began to run in different directions. She had to be careful here. She had no clue about what Karen was getting at. Trying to ignore the other girl, Jill pushed herself out of her uniform. It caught on her running shoe. The crowd of hairs were doing aerobics on her legs.

"I think there's some thrill in this legs competition for you," drawled Karen.

Something hid behind her words. Slow, Jill thought. Don't reach for your sweatshirt too quick. She can smell fear.

"How come you don't ever take a shower here, Jill?" asked Karen.

Caught on its label, her sweatshirt would not come off its

hook. Jill pulled at it, and it tore loose. Inside the sweatshirt, she paused. Her head and arms did not really want to find their way back out, but she had to resurface sometime. As Jill's face emerged, she found Karen three inches away from her left shoulder. The girl stood there, casual in her underwear and cleavage. Jill fought the desire to jump away.

"What d' you want?" Jill whispered.

"What do *I* want?" said Karen. Her tone smiled.

Jill could not look at her. "Yeah."

"What do I want?" Karen mused. There was a pause. "We're a little worried about you, Jill. You've been acting odd. This concerns us." She ducked down, traced a finger along the hair on Jill's lower left leg. "Tsk, tsk."

"Yeah, really," said someone else.

"Like, for sure," said another.

Karen straightened. "Well, I'm going to take a shower now," she drawled. "Maybe we should be glad you don't want to join us in the shower, eh, Jill? A little safer—for us, I mean." She moved past Jill, leaving about one quarter inch to spare.

THE P.A. CRACKLED between announcements. Rob had just finished enthusiastically blabbing her first-place finish in the girls section of the chess competition to the entire school. Jill refused to look up.

A second PA voice cleared itself of gravel and nerves.

"Coach Booth here. Just reminding you of the Lovely Legs Competition. Forms are available in the next *Telegraph* issue. C'mon out and show your school spirit. And have a little fun."

This time, Jill did look up. All around her, kids continued to sit motionless between their ears. Nobody seemed to have heard the announcement or noticed its implications. Jill wondered: If I screamed very, very long and very, very loud, would anyone notice?

She picked her binder up, held it three feet above the floor and dropped it. It was a satisfying sudden epidemic of noise, producing the desired effect: turned heads, oversized eyes and gaping mouths. Jill was relieved. Their ears worked.

"Too bad about their brains," His Eminence chuckled.

"Oh, sorry," said Jill. She bent down and picked up her binder.

AS SHE ROUNDED the landing stairwell, Jill saw Dwayne and Liza. Liza's hair was pulled back in a barrette, and she had on a red sweater. It made her face seem warmer. Yesterday, she had worn yellow. Jill slid in between their hellos. They surrounded her like a pocket.

"Did you bring my lunch?" asked Dwayne. "I forgot it."

Smugness outlined Jill's smile. "Mom asked me to, but I forgot."

Dwayne looked glum.

"Sorry," said Jill. "Want a lifesaver? Butterscotch—my favorite."

Liza laughed. It was such a glad new sound, coming from her. Jill counted it a personal triumph.

"Here," said Jill. "You can have one of my sandwiches."

"Marmalade?" frowned Dwayne.

"This one has black currant jam," said Jill. "From Poland."

"Oh," said Dwayne, relieved. He took the sandwich.

"I heard something about you today, Jill," said Liza. She licked at some peanut butter that was escaping her bread. Lately, she had been eating peanut butter and relish sandwiches.

"A-out ee?" asked Jill. She was also eating peanut butter.

"They were talking about your legs," said Liza.

"About the competition?" asked Dwayne.

"No," said Liza.

"The hair?" said Jill.

"Hair?" said Dwayne.

"Hair," said Liza.

Dwayne's head continued to rotate between the two of them in search of explanations. Jill was wary. They had left that long-ago backyard confrontation in the backyard. They also seemed to have left a lot of the Two People They Turned Into Next To Each Other somewhere back in the past. But you never knew.

"About five, six weeks ago," she explained, "I decided to stop shaving my legs. I only have two legs. That doesn't make a majority in this place. Doesn't force anyone else to copy me to stay in style or something. But it seems to have caused a pandemonium of thought."

"Oh," grunted Dwayne. He picked up her third sandwich. Jill was about to protest, then remembered that it was marmalade. She would get it back.

"Well, why're you doing this?" Dwayne asked. "It's kind of a weird thing to do, don't you think?"

"You're right," said Jill. "It is a weird thing to do—shaving our legs. Why did we start? And why do we keep doing it?"

"Because it looks better," said Dwayne. He bit into her sandwich. A betrayed look crossed his face and the sandwich was deposited in her lap, minus much of its center.

"You have an overbite," Jill said.

"I do not," replied Dwayne.

"Then a big mouth," she insisted. "And you took all the marmalade."

"Then I left the edible stuff," he said. "Give it back."

Jill shoved the rest of the sandwich into her mouth.

"Pig," he said. "Look, what d' you want on your legs? Long goat hairs trailing all over the place?"

Jill swallowed seven times in rapid succession and managed to get most of the bread crust down. "Well, you've got hair on your legs."

"That's right—I got guy's legs," answered Dwayne. "D' you want to have guy's legs?"

Jill pulled her sweat pant legs up to her knees, then pushed down her knee socks. "Y' see—look. Is that so awful?" The hairs stood straight up from the friction. They looked as enthusiastic as cheerleaders.

"They look like skinny guy's legs," said Dwayne. "You're not a guy."

"This is the way my legs are supposed to look," protested Jill. "Natural, not hairy. Natural."

"Look," said Dwayne. Pulling down his socks, he exposed about three inches of ankle. He placed one foot close to Jill's. "You've got hairier ankles than I do."

It was true. Dwayne had next to no hair around his ankles. This, Jill thought, is the last straw.

Liza started to laugh again, quite clearly, almost like a handbell. Jill and Dwayne observed each other so close that their noses almost touched. "You're very weird, Jill," said Dwayne. "Your brain is on overdrive too much. The battery's running out. You gonna stop using deodorant, too?"

Liza sniffed through her giggles. "I can see your point, Jill."

Jill shoved Dwayne triumphantly. "I sure wish you were in my gym class, Liza."

"Drop it," advised Liza. "I did."

"How'd you get out of it?" asked Jill.

"My psychiatrist wrote me a note," said Liza. She savored the texture of the word as she said it. *Psychiatrist.* Probably she had been unsure whether to let it out of her mouth. "You don't mind if I see a psychiatrist, do you?"

Jill felt her own hesitation and hated it.

"No!" Dwayne's answer was so decisive it punched a hole into the air.

Liza ducked her head down momentarily. Then she looked at Jill and grinned. "If you want to get out of gym, I could get you an appointment."

Dwayne snorted.

"I'd almost go for that," said Jill. "It's not as funny as you think." No one seemed to notice her mood change, though His Eminence raised an eyebrow. She shrugged at him.

Dwayne shifted. "What's it like, going to a psychiatrist? Like, what do you talk about?"

"That's kind of personal, Dwayne," said Jill.

"Oh, that's okay," said Liza. "Mostly she wants to know how my medication is going."

"Drugs?" grinned Dwayne. "Happy drugs?"

"Sleepy drugs," said Liza. "Want some?"

"For the nights Dwayne snores," said Jill. "I'd like to shove them up his nose. Sounds like a motorcycle."

"I told her about you two," said Liza.

"About your super awesome majorly supreme protection?" asked Dwayne.

"She thought you sounded really nice," said Liza. "I told her she was right."

Jill saw her brother flush. She felt rather warm herself. She pulled down her pant leg, leaned briefly, happily, against her brother's shoulder.

"Aw, shucks," she said.

DWAYNE WATCHED JILL pull out *The Mission* CD.

"Are you going to bawl for the next hour?" he demanded.

"Yup."

"Why?"

Jill put the words carefully. "Why do you take care of Liza?" She put in the CD, and the music began to cut its fine painful line.

Dwayne was staring at the floor. "Well, it's not because I want to hurt myself . . . make myself unhappy."

"But you know you do," said Jill. "Every time you're with her, you hurt. I've watched you."

"You figure, eh?"

"I figure," said Jill. She turned from the awareness in his eyes.

"At least she's alive, though," he muttered. "She's here and now. This movie is about something that happened hundreds of years back."

"Yeah, I know." It was starting to snow outside. Jill watched it come down. "But it's alive in me, I guess."

He frowned. "Don't you think, maybe, you listen to it too much?"

Jill shrugged. "Maybe."

Dwayne sighed. "Well, if you're gonna put those shrieking singers on, I'm going upstairs." He left.

Jill turned the volume up.

JILL WAS HELPING Ewald collate the November issue of the *Telegraph*. He was very quiet. Jill figured too much bureaucratic pollution had gotten into his brain. But that was fine with her—she was planning on stapling an extra piece of paper to each *Telegraph* copy after he left.

Yesterday, she had photocopied her black market survey about the Lovely Legs Competition and sexism. It had been discouraging, trudging around the school, going from mind to mind and getting the same response with minimal variations—WHO CARES?! Nobody except Cal, a few teachers and several of the older girls questioned it at all. Unsure if she could face their responses, she had not asked Dwayne or Liza. She wondered what Peter would have said. She sighed. That's what she was these days—a series of sighs. A sigh serial.

She had not bothered with the cafeteria survey. She hoped Ewald thought she was helping him collate as penance. "So," she said, trying for the third time to whip up a conversation. "What d' you think about reincarnation? Ewald—you're unbuttoning your shirt again."

Ewald buttoned up the top buttons. "Jill, I should tell you 'bout something, but I don't really know how to say it."

"Oh," said Jill. Ewald had displayed a two-button nervousness. Mediocre apprehension, she evaluated. "So shoot. My ears are expanding."

"Well . . . this isn't me. This is just other people, and even though I told them they couldn't, I still think you should know, because it's about you, and I think you'd rather know than not. Being in the dark isn't much fun, and then, when all of a sudden, someone turns the light on, you feel kind of like—"

"Ewald," said Jill. "Turn the light on."

"Well, they don't want you in the legs competition," stammered Ewald. "I couldn't help it—it's them."

"Who's 'them'?"

"It's these girls," sighed Ewald. "They got a petition going. All the other girls in the competition signed it."

Jill wished the hot balloon expanding in her stomach would blow up. "What's their problem? I can't be that much competition."

"I guess they figure you're trying to make fun of them, Jill." Ewald was stapling with meticulous care.

"Trying to make fun of them?" Jill had not expected this. Those girls were brighter than she had imagined. But then, why had they entered the competition? Jill had figured it was because they were low-functioning, had a one-size-fits-all IQ. "So does that mean I'm out of the competition?"

"No," said Ewald. "I don't think anyone can stop you from entering. There's no rule that says you have to shave your legs to enter." He stopped piling papers and leaned on his hands, staring down at the desk. He sighed. "Y' know Jill, I don't know why, but ever since you started all this stuff about the competition, you've made me feel really guilty. Every time you walk into a room, every time I think of you, I feel . . . guilty. Like I should've done something, or I should-n't have done something. Y' know?"

Jill stared at him. "I don't get it. I never said anything to you."

Ewald began unbuttoning again. "Well, it's like this: I did-n't give a damn about that competition. It was just an idea I had one day after I heard some kids joking around."

"So you approached my brother," Jill said.

"Yeah. I approached your brother. He and his friends thought it would be great. They wanted it. I gave it to them. That's what my job is—make 'em happy." He gave a nostal-gic sigh. "Everyone was happy. Then you came along and made me feel like I should be throwing myself in front of cars to stop the Miss America Pageant or something. I got enough on my mind just running this newspaper, Jill."

"I'm sorry," said Jill. "I didn't mean to make you feel that way."

"Well, that's the whole thing," said Ewald. "I know it's not your fault, but it's still happening. Y' see, I know it's *my* problem. Don't you see? When you walk into a room, all of a sudden, I see *my* problem."

"Oh, great," cried Jill. "Now I'm a magnifying glass."

Ewald swallowed and went on to the next button. "Well, I wouldn't have mentioned it, but I don't think it's just me. Y' see, I think that's what's behind this petition. You got all those girls thinking they're stupid or they're wrong or they don't have any brains because they want to be in this competition."

"That'd be about right," muttered Jill.

"Maybe they've thought that about themselves all along," said Ewald. "I think, most of the time, I'm pretty much the nerd so I do the nerd things, like run the *Telegraph*. I kind of stay out of things where I might not do as well. The days I hated phys. ed. the most, in my head, I corrected the grammar on every word that came out of Coach's mouth. Those girls . . . maybe all their . . . " He blushed. "All their clothes and fashion stuff is for the same reason. You make them feel like they're not good enough, Jill."

Ewald began sorting papers again. "Look, I felt kind of stupid saying that, but I thought maybe you'd rather know than not know, y' know what I mean?"

"Yeah," said Jill. "I know what you mean."

She turned and left. There was a large garbage pail down the hallway. Slowly, she tipped her survey copies into it and walked away.

JILL LOCKED herself into the bathroom, hoping no one else in the house had been drinking very many fluids; she figured she would be in there for a while. As the cold water ran, she stared into the mirror. What if everyone thought the way Ewald did? Was she really one massive guilt trip for the entire school population? She splashed water on her face, then came up for another look.

Things looked kind of blurry when you cried this much.

Jill placed her nose against the mirror's surface, trying to see her eyes more clearly. She frowned. Two faces were there in the glass. One, she thought, was her own. Around it hovered another, slightly larger. It was His Eminence. The legate sat in the mirror, looking back at her.

Jill pulled back sharply from the mirror and blinked. When she moved cautiously close to the mirror again, His Eminence had disappeared, leaving one face, swollen and very confused. "Mega Warp, kid," it said to her. "You're losing it, Hollywood style."

JILL PULLED her black sweater over her head and shivered as cold air took its place. She reached for the blue cotton uniform. She felt quite proud of herself—today she had remembered to bring an under-the-poverty-line version of the fashionable white sweat socks.

Suddenly, a finger slid under her bra strap, scraping her back with the fingernail. The elastic tightened painfully under her breasts. Whoever it was, she had pulled the strap well back. It was released and snapped back into place. There was laughter.

Jill straightened her bra, which had been pulled askew. Her hands shook. Her head made a rattling noise. Maybe that was why the floor rolled around in waves. Dressed only in her underwear, it was too hard to turn and face the girls. She reached for the blue uniform again. This time, a hand pulled the uniform away. As Jill grabbed for it, the uniform was whipped out of sight.

"Bet you it smells," said a voice. "Bet you it reeks. Stinks like a lez."

Jill put one hand out to touch her locker door. Something had to be real. The voice continued.

"Hey, lez, how's the hair crop you're growing on your legs?"

Later, Jill wondered who it was that took over her body for the next seven or eight seconds. Her arm swung around, heavy and mighty as a steel crane, and her body followed.

She saw her hands reach out, big as concrete blocks and full of some black meaning. She had a blurred vision of a girl holding the uniform. Then the two hands at the ends of Jill's arms shoved into this girl's shoulders so that she banged loudly against a locker. Jill grabbed her uniform back. Her legs had mutated to a tough rubber, but they managed to step over the bench, banging an insole. It did not hurt until later. Her body was stiff and thick, immense in size. Jill stalked to the washroom, went into a cubicle and locked the door.

She shook so badly, she could hardly get the uniform on. Buttoning it up, Jill noticed a torn shoulder. It seemed a good enough reason to cry, so she sat on the toilet and sobbed.

For most of the gym period, Jill walked. She went to her hall locker, put on her coat and left through the front door. She could not go home; she had agreed to meet Dwayne and Liza at the basketball game after classes. Dwayne was not playing because of a sprained ankle. Though it was snowing, she kept her hood down. She wanted the touch of the tiny cold fingerprints on her hot face. Gradually, the throbbing behind her eyelids lessened. She could breathe more easily. His Eminence hovered on one side of her brain, but she ignored him. She did not want to think.

Jill stood, head dropped back and eyes closed. A sweet coolness came tiptoeing through her. She stood still, not wanting to disturb it, not wanting to ruffle the tenuous interior. The snowflakes were lovely, large and drifting down in clumps. If only ideas fell out of the grey sky like that—white and delicate, settling on eyelashes and hair, dissolving on the tongue, in the cave of the ear. If ideas fell like snowflakes, everyone would be kept busy just watching them come down, examining each new pattern. But no, she thought after a moment. Sounded nice, but it was too idealistic. If ideas were snowflakes, sooner or later they'd get packed into snowballs so people could fire them at one another.

Hair damp about her face, Jill walked back to the school.

Maybe she was overdoing it. She had every right to decide for herself, but maybe she was interfering with the opinions of others. Maybe she would just drop out of that stupid competition.

She hung up her coat in her locker and walked to the gym. The game was in progress. She located Dwayne standing at one side to the back, both hands cupped to his mouth, yelling. Liza was next to him, shoulders hunched. Dwayne had talked her into coming to this game, had been giving her a series of pep talks all week. Now Liza seemed almost to be shrinking into herself as she watched the people around her. Jill started toward them.

She saw Dwayne turn to Liza, say something to her and then duck down behind her. Jill knew he meant to give Liza a better view by hoisting her up onto his shoulders. Shit, she thought. Bad idea, Dwayne.

Jill began to run. By the time she reached them, Liza was screaming. She hit and kicked at Dwayne, who was trying to get his arms around her to hold her still. He looked dazed and confused.

"Let her go," Jill bawled into his ear, pulling at his shoulder.

Dwayne let go. Crying, Liza backed away, then turned and ran from the gym.

"Don't move," Jill ordered her brother. "I'll go talk to her."

Jill paused at the inner doorway to the nearest girls washroom. She could hear Liza in a cubicle, doubled over and vomiting into a toilet. "Liza?"

What the hell was she supposed to do or say? Jill wondered. How could something that happened in the past be more real to Liza than the people around her now? How come she did not just get over it? "Liza?"

Liza came out of the cubicle. She went to one of the sinks and began washing her face. Slowly, Jill walked over and handed her a paper towel. Without looking at her, Liza wiped her face and threw the towel in the garbage. She stood, tracing her finger through the water puddles on the sink.

"Just an hour ago," said Jill, "I was sitting on the toilet in the girls locker room, bawling my head off. Funny thing."

Liza looked at her sideways. "Jill." Her voice wobbled. "Dwayne's the nicest guy I've ever met. He must hate me. He must feel stupid."

"He would do anything for you, Liza," Jill said fiercely. "God. Don't say those kinds of things. Don't even think them. Dwayne made a mistake. He forgot you were nervous. It was just a mistake. He won't do it again. He wanted to help you see better, that's all."

"I know that now." Liza's hand fluttered to her throat. "There was so much noise and so many people jumping and screaming and moving so fast. I didn't hear what he said." Her face wrenched out of shape. "And then he touched my legs."

"Yeah, I know," murmured Jill.

"He won't think I'm an idiot?"

"No!" said Jill vehemently. "Nobody thinks that."

"Some people do," said Liza. "I know they do. But you don't. Maybe Dwayne won't?"

"He absolutely does not."

There was a pause.

"D' you want me to go home with you now?" asked Jill.

"No," said Liza. "I want to go back." There was a smile on her mouth, in her eyes.

"Yeeeeeee-ess," said Jill. "This is gonna be a good game. We're gonna win. I can feel it in my bones, my corpuscles, my nuclei!"

Suddenly, Jill withdrew her decision to withdraw from the Lovely Legs Competition. For the second time, she put her arm around Liza's shoulders. Liza did not even flinch.

His Eminence was watching the Guaraní sing. When Jill closed her eyes, she saw his still face under its heavy wig, just inside her lids. Every time she blinked, he was there for a second. That moment of dark between the longer moments of light had been invaded, taken over. Now it was His Eminence's face.

"Your reasons were wrong," she told him. "You were cruel. You let them all die. You, in your white robes—such a good disguise for black—you were wrong."

"Look at the flip side," His Eminence said suddenly. "Two sides to every coin, Jill."

"What flip side?"

But she had interrupted him. His Eminence returned his gaze to the Guaraní. Inside her head, the natives kept singing.

MEDUSA FACE

New posters were all over the school now. With three
weeks to go until the competition, the whole school
seemed wallpapered in pink.

Jill had checked the list of competitors in Ewald's Editor's
Binder. It had lengthened to twenty-five names and was
composed of Karen and Arlene, and visual echoes of Karen
and Arlene . . . and Jill. As she ate lunch in the stairwell, one
of the posters glared down at her.

"Look at this poster," complained Jill.

"It's got some pretty good-looking legs on it," commented Dwayne. "I like the mistletoe around the ankles."

"They look like leftovers from automobile accidents,"
protested Jill. "There aren't any bodies attached to them."

"Why did you *really* enter, Jill?" asked Liza.

Jill noticed Dwayne suddenly bend down and begin to
retie a shoelace. There was still, sometimes, this stain of confusion between them. "I thought hairy legs would be . . .
some sort of statement," she shrugged.

Dwayne grunted, but Liza looked interested. As long as
she wanted to listen, Dwayne would have to, too. Still, Jill
hesitated. To *really* talk about this without throwing out a
joke as decoy? It would make her feel like a TV evangelist.

"It's not like I expected all the girls in the school to immediately say, 'Oh. Now I understand the true meaning of leg hair. The ultimate meaning of women's legs is hairiness.' I just didn't want to sit in the middle of the audience at that competition like everybody else—part of one big assumption."

"Worried about your image?" Dwayne stood up.

"What image?"

Dwayne looked away, restless, as Jill waited for his response. Finally, he shrugged.

"That competition is just one wrong move in the middle of a whole bunch of other wrong moves," Jill said. "They go on all the time, Dwayne. Y' know, like I'm supposed to wear shoulder pads because my shoulders don't look good enough on their own. I'm supposed to wear lipstick because my lips aren't the right color. Like, forget it. I'm a girl, and I am the way a girl is. I don't have to read a magazine to find out how I should be. I just am."

Dwayne glanced out the window. There was a pause. It pushed against them. Jill pushed back.

"I don't have to enter that legs competition to find out if my legs are good enough."

"Well, if you know they're good enough, why're you entering?" Dwayne sounded impatient. He would not listen to much more of this.

"Just to be there," replied Jill. "Just to be there, I think . . . and to say, in the middle of it all, it doesn't have to be this way. An option, y' know?"

Dwayne's hand followed the twists of the stair railing. "If it's not going to make a difference, why bother? I mean, of course you've got the right. Every girl in the school could do what you're doing. But they aren't. So it must not matter very much to them. Geez, Jill—this isn't South Africa."

Liza stirred a plastic spoon round and round her yogurt container. She spoke slowly, watching the pineapple chunks. "I think," she said. "I wish . . ." Her eyes looked into Jill with the weight of that afternoon in the October rain, that afternoon Dwayne still knew nothing about. "I wish I had the guts."

Jill remembered Liza huddled on the ground, the puddles that grew with each raindrop. Her eyes stung, and she looked away.

Inside her head was a white movement. His Eminence stirred and looked at her. It was weird. Jill saw Liza when her eyes opened, His Eminence when they closed.

"Nice thing, this feeling of power, eh, Jill?" he said and grinned.

EWALD WAS WAITING next to her locker. "Jill." Anxiety hovered about him like invisible angel wings, ready to lift him off the ground at any moment.

"Yes?" Jill fiddled with her combination lock. Ewald's nerves were tangling her thoughts. Was it twenty-six, twelve, two? Two, twelve, twenty-six?

"Jill—we're not going to have room for a survey in the next issue."

She was not sure what this meant. She kept her eyes lowered.

"Coach wants us to run an entry form in each issue, so your space'll be taken up," he explained.

Her eyelids felt very heavy. "Oh."

"So, um, there's not really a point in coming to the next meeting, Jill. Y' know, they're pretty boring, and there isn't anything for you to do, y' know?"

"Oh."

"So, see ya." A black hole appeared and sucked Ewald away. In just a little while, Jill moved again. Yes, she could remember her combination now. Twelve, two, twenty-six.

"JILL'S ON OUR TEAM TODAY," SAID KAREN.

She stood behind Jill, tying and retying the strings of an orange bib at the back of Jill's neck. Large soundless glaciers were gliding through Jill's stomach. Karen patted her shoulder.

"Let's make her feel like one of us," Karen continued. "Part of the team. Maybe that's why Jill has so many problems. She feels like she's not one of us."

Jill wanted to employ some variation of the primal scream. The group of girls watched her. All of them had Karen's eyes. Jill stared back. This was *Lord of the Flies* on the basketball court. "I'm all right," she said.

"Okay," said Karen. "Remember, the ball goes to Jill."

"No," said Jill. "I . . . "

They had all turned away. The whistle shrieked.

"Where's your missing player?" asked Ms. Cottrell.

"Oh, that's Jill," called Karen. Blond ponytail flipping back and forth, she ran on the spot, warming up. She looked like an exercise video.

"C'mon, Jill," rasped the coach.

Inside her head was another white movement. "They're coming for you," said His Eminence. He looked very serious, in a buddy-buddy sort of way. It was hard to take with the wig. Jill swallowed. Sweat ran down her inner arms.

"C'mon, Jill," repeated the coach. The whistle shrieked again.

In jerky movements, Jill walked onto the court. She felt miles above the tops of her legs, her feet very far away. Where did the forward position stand? Over there, where there was a large vacant space of floor without a blue cotton uniform to fill it. The whistle screamed.

Jill stood, trying to remember who was on her team. She looked down at her bib. It was orange. Oh, yes, the other team wore green bibs. So many orange and green bibs out there moving around. Suddenly, a ball showed up, a perfect shoulder pass. Jill warded it off her throat. It slammed her hands against her chest. She stood, ball in her hands.

"Jill!" It was Karen. Jill threw the ball at her. It wobbled through the air until a green bib snatched it.

Jill tried to fade back down the court, closer to her own basket. She was good at this, had fine-tuned her avoidance technique. But then she heard the ball thudding down the floor. Green bibs swooped around her. She turned and the ball slammed into her abdomen and pushed everything out.

"Jill!" It was Karen.

Jill tried to get some air in around the concrete wall in her lungs. All she wanted was a sliver of air. It was such a relief when Karen took the enormous weight of the ball away.

Jill decided to stay by her team's basketball hoop. But suddenly they were coming back. The ball was being dribbled back to the net by her own team. Someone sent a bounce pass. It leaped up from the floor, jamming the end of her fourth finger. Jill dropped the ball, pain ramming her hand. But she had to get the ball and throw it back to them. Then they'd leave her alone for a bit. She ignored the pain and grabbed at the ball. She had it.

Karen was beside her, and someone hovered behind— someone else from her team. "Dribble—we'll cover you."

There were orange bibs on either side, their elbows so close. Green bibs advanced toward her, blocking her way. Jill concentrated on bouncing the ball. That way she didn't have to watch them all coming at her. Karen moved in closer, her arm brushing against Jill's. The breathing of the girl behind grew louder. They were all closing in on her, wanting the ball. The ball—what was she supposed to do with the ball?

"Take it," she hissed at Karen.

There was no answer. All around her, bodies were squeezing her in.

Out. She needed out.

Jill threw the ball straight up into the air. Karen's elbow dug into her side. Knees behind Jill's pushed at her, bending her own forward. A green bib slammed into her chest. Finally, everything stopped.

Ms. Cottrell leaned over her. The ceiling went around her face like the brim of a hat. "I think you'd better sit this next one out, Jill," she said. "Basketball just isn't your thing."

"No," said Jill.

The other girls were standing up. She could see their legs shift around her. Everyone else would be all right. They had all landed on top of her. The floor would be fine, too. Her own body? Nothing broken. Nothing to write home about.

"Just a sore knee," Jill told the coach, adding silently, and a few elbow-sized bruises for decoration.

As she hobbled to the bench, His Eminence observed, "This time was easy. Keep an eye out for the future, kiddo."

GROGGY FROM A LATE-NIGHT SESSION with His Eminence and *The Mission* soundtrack, Jill found her seat in Latin next to the window. Somebody had to keep an eye on the smoking club, waylay its plans to destroy the ozone layer. Behind her, the seat was empty. So Deb had not arrived yet.

Yes, she had. She was sitting on the other side of the class, behind Berthwalda Lutic. Bernice, actually. They had dubbed her Berthwalda for no real reason, other than a rather substantial nose. Jill had done the dubbing. Not very nice, she supposed. And now she was surrounded by eight empty desks.

She had thought Deb would always be there, just like everything else that fell under the category of mundane. Solitude was heavy.

She heard Deb giggle, say something to Greg Sacuta. It would be best to look down at her desk, Jill decided.

JILL STARED at the CD cover. She understood, now, why the music made her cry. It was just that everything was changing—all around her, nothing the same. The music was like that—always moving. It was so beautiful inside her it hurt, and then it ended, leaving her alone. Alone.

So much changing. If even one thing would stay the same, just for a while. But then, maybe she would not recognize it. She could not seem to remember the way things had been, before . . . before everything had started to go wrong like this.

The voices sang, cutting deeper. Jill reached over and turned the stereo off.

JILL WALKED into the cafeteria. Fatigue was rolling around in her head, and she had a Latin test next class. Chocolate milk and a root beer—that might get those verbs conjugating in proper form again.

From a table to her left, a voice called, "Hey, lez."

Jill tried to ignore the laughter and moved on without turning her head.

"Hey, lez, where're you going? Hey, Jill Gilbert! Come back here, you lez."

If Jill had been able to think, she would have. There was a blur of stairs, windows, lockers, then some cold air and she was on the street, running for home.

No one was in the house. She thought she had finished crying three times before, finally, the air moved in to cradle her like a baby. She slept.

HIS EMINENCE HAD FOUND a pair of white sweats. He had pulled them up to his knees and was studying his leg hair, his white wig slightly askew. "Excuse me," muttered Jill, "but this is not your problem."

She placed the CD in the player and turned up the volume. Beauty and pain, beauty and pain. She needed the reminder that they traveled together, all mixed up, one the deeper current of the other.

"Y' know, I looked up your singing Guaraní in the encyclopedia," Jill told him. "The movie didn't get all of it right. It's alleged that they were a warlike people who took captives and ate them."

His Eminence ignored this. He had started to count the number of hairs on one leg. "One, two, three, four . . . " His low voice went on and on. Good grief, Jill moaned silently. She knew this would go on for hours.

"GOT A PENNY, LIZA?" ASKED JILL.

They were walking the tracks. Dwayne kicked at the gravel along the embankment.

"I used to flatten nickels to use as quarters in slot machines," said Liza. "What d' you want a penny for?"

Dwayne looked up. "To derail a train. Here, I got one."

Jill caught the penny he tossed her and laid the copper on the steel rail. Cold clung to their faces, and their words were haunted by a white vapor. They had been ambling along slowly, adding miles to their talk.

"Wonder if old Queen Liz feels it as the wheels flatten her face," said Jill. "Maybe she gets a sudden fear Quebec will opt out of the Commonwealth."

Dwayne lit another cigarette. "I think a freight comes through around 4:15. Let's wait and see it crush our fortunes."

Jill stepped up onto one of the rails, and her runner slid on its curved edges. Liza stepped up, too, careful to avoid the penny. Cigarette dangling from his lips, Dwayne balanced on the opposite rail, facing them. Liza was better at balance than she or Dwayne, Jill realized.

"Y' know the story about Medusa?" asked Liza. Her arms wobbled, outstretched. "She's the one who can turn you to stone by looking at you. Her hair's made of snakes."

"Jill in the morning," grunted Dwayne.

"Thanks," said Jill.

Liza's dark hair was damp. It cupped her face, and her cheekbones were ridged more sharply than usual. "D' you ever get the feeling," she asked, "that every person turns into a Medusa?"

"What d' you mean?" asked Dwayne, pulling the cigarette from his mouth.

"Like in a daydream," said Liza. "When I think about someone, they smile and walk away. Then suddenly, they turn around and their face is different. It was normal. It was nice. They turn around and it's changed."

Dwayne studied Liza carefully. Almost, thought Jill, as if he were washing a window between them, trying to get a better view. I watch you, she thought, and you watch her. This is the way we are. She walked slowly away from them, balancing, half listening to the conversation.

Ahead, at the Edinburgh crossing, the signal sounded. Jill saw the train coming around the bend. It fit November's art scheme—the blacks, greys, browns. Even the reds were rusty, as if they had forgotten sunlight. Any light hitting the train's sides would be swallowed, sucked under its surface.

This was an odd feeling. A bit like a dream. The train came on, soundless, like a TV screen with the volume turned down. Someone had turned on the Guaraní. They were singing in her head. The voices wove in and out of one other. They moved so fast. She had to keep absolutely still, listen and pay attention so she would not lose any of their movement, that movement of sound all around her. Otherwise the voices would get too far ahead of her and vanish, leaving her alone like they always did.

The voices swelled, huge with the coming of the train. It took away the sky, filled her eyes, and all she wanted to do was stand there, small and straight, unmoving. The singing grew louder. Jill stood straight up, resisting. Resist the train. Let it come closer. Closer. It was so big now, its sound rushed into her ears, its smell into her nose, filling her head.

Something knocked Jill's shoulder, and the ground slammed into her rib cage. Then the sky was squeezed out of her eyes. A circle pushed through her forehead and into her head, twirling around and around, around and around. She opened her eyes. Tree branches hung onto the edges of the sky, but they were teasing her, shifting as if in a high wind. There was a loud roaring, a sudden diminuendo. The train was gone.

Then she heard the sound of Dwayne's voice. He was yelling, his two hands shaking her shoulders against the ground. She smelled the smoke of his cigarette.

"You goddamn idiot!" he yelled.

He pulled at her, trying, Jill assumed, to get her to stand. The sky swung away, and she saw a hedge waver just beyond his scowling face. The air felt like cold entrails in her nose. She pushed Dwayne away.

"What's your problem?" Groggy, Jill stood up. Trees square danced. "What happened?"

He was still yelling. "You would've been dead if I hadn't pulled you off that rail!" Breathing hard, he stared at her. Blue eyes took up half his face.

Jill remembered the feeling of the train getting bigger and bigger. The shriek, the vibrations, the way it took over her head. "I guess I kind of blanked out," she muttered.

"Christ." Dwayne's voice shook. "Maybe we *should* send you to a psychiatrist. That's all I need—another case to take care of."

The words cut through the haze packaging Jill's brain. She shoved at him, hard, pushing against his largeness, the way it loomed over her. He did not yield but dropped the cigarette and wrapped his arms around her, an angry grip that did not let her breathe.

"Fuck you," Jill muttered into his coat. Tears burned her face.

Dwayne shoved her aside and stooped down. He picked up the flattened penny and held up its dull defaced gleam at the end of her nose. Then he forced it, thin and cold, into her hand. "D' you get it yet?"

She pushed at him again. He was too close to her face. "Where's Liza? She heard you say that, y' know—about the psychiatrist. We gotta find her."

They walked for ten minutes in silence, searching, then spotted Liza across a field hemmed by apartment buildings. Quickly, Dwayne began to run toward her.

"If you run, she'll run," Jill called after him. Stupid idiot, she thought, fatigue pulling at her. She saw Liza begin to run as Dwayne neared her, but he caught at her wrist, holding her there until she stopped pulling.

"Let's go to Tim Hortons," said Jill, when she reached them. "I'm cold."

"Let me go," said Liza.

"Please," said Dwayne.

THE RESTAURANT'S WARMTH seeped into Jill's skin. She and Liza found a seat by the window and left Dwayne to do the ordering. Liza had been crying. Jill had been crying. It was getting repetitious.

Why wasn't I afraid of that train? she wondered. Dwayne

sat down next to Liza and shoved coffees and doughnuts on waxed paper at them.

"You're the one who likes apple fritters," Jill pointed out.

"If you don't like it, I'll eat it," replied Dwayne. He lit a cigarette.

"I thought you only smoked occasionally," muttered Jill.

"This is certainly an occasion," he said, staring past her out the window. His hand shook. Liza did not touch her coffee or doughnut.

"You trying to kill yourself?" asked Dwayne abruptly.

"No," Jill mumbled. She poured two creamers and two sugars into her coffee. Half of them made it into the mug. Slowly, she stirred the coffee with a brown plastic stick.

"So what if you were?" It was the first thing Liza had said. The words were cool, clear. "I've tried it a coupla times. Got caught once. The other times just didn't work out."

Jill watched her brother set his cigarette in the ash tray, then rub his face slowly with both hands. He left red marks on his forehead.

"Well," continued Liza, "I guess I am a case. Maybe we should all stop pretending that you two wonderful kids with your wonderful parents will rescue me from my bad dreams."

Liza cradled the coffee cup with her hands.

"What did you want me to turn into? The captain of the debating team? Maybe I'm tired of having to be something for you. Maybe I don't want to talk to people. Maybe I'd rather sit in corners by myself. Maybe I just don't want to be what you want me to be."

"Well, maybe we started off by trying to help," stammered Jill. Dwayne had not taken his hands from his face and sat very still. "But now, you're a friend. We like you. You're . . . you're a friend." The words wobbled out of her mouth, not strong enough to carry their own weight.

"You heard him," said Liza. "I'm another case. Someone you need to take care of. Are you relieved when you drop me off at my front door?" She turned to Dwayne. "I know they call you my baby-sitter."

"What?" asked Jill.

"Nobody pays me by the hour," said Dwayne. "I wouldn't do this if I didn't want to."

"Give me a cigarette," said Liza.

"What d' you mean, baby-sitter?" said Jill. "Nobody calls me your baby-sitter."

Dwayne pushed the cigarette pack at Liza. "No, it's me. The team, y' know?"

"I didn't invite you to hang out with me," said Liza. She pulled out a cigarette and lit it with one of Dwayne's matches. She inhaled, then swore softly. "You have no idea," she said. "Almost every time I'm talking to you two . . . you have no idea. You're talking away about your wonderful mom and your wonderful dad, or the basketball team, or some chess tournament you just played in. You're thinking about how you're improving my life, the whole time. I can feel you thinking it. Yes—still."

Liza directed this at Jill, then sucked on the cigarette, hollows defining her cheeks.

"You feel so good about this. And the whole time, I'm sitting here, just trying to keep my guts together. Sometimes, the floor is gone underneath, and I'm falling. I'm scared—shitless, all of a sudden. Like that." She snapped her fingers. "For no reason. Like, this hole opens up in my guts, and it sucks in my face and my arms and my head. All of a sudden, they're just sucked down into it. They disappear. And both your faces—they turn into Medusa faces. And you're both just talking away. Shit, you have no idea."

"What do we do to make that happen?" asked Jill.

"Nothing," said Liza. "That's the point. It just does. It could happen any minute now. Y' see, I am a case. Ask my psychiatrist."

Dwayne turned and looked at Liza. "I don't give a shit about the football team. And I don't give a shit about the basketball team. Yeah, my parents are great. We got a good deal there. But sometimes . . . " He stopped, started again. "Sometimes, I don't know what to say to you. So much has changed. I'm just this football case. I do good on the field. I know how to stop what's coming at me, how to get what I want. I don't know how to get it for you, Liza. I want to—" His words snapped off, midsentence.

"God," muttered Liza. "Everyone crying like this." She pulled at the serviette container, ripping the first napkin. "Here." She handed it to Dwayne, pulled a second one out for herself. Then, looking at Jill, she pulled a third. The three of them wiped their faces, laughing in small gulps.

"You're not a case," said Dwayne. "I'm the case. Here I could've saved myself a life-long nuisance, but I had to go and save Jill."

"Lucky you didn't have enough time to really think about it, eh?" asked Jill.

"I was just kidding."

"Me, too." But there was an edge to Jill's smile.

"THE IDEA IS NEVER to let a *real* train run you down, Jill," said His Eminence. "You want to live to see the symbolic value of your actions as an aftersight."

"I wasn't trying to kill myself," protested Jill. "It just happened. I just kind of blanked out. I thought I heard singing."

"You're getting your metaphors mixed," commented His Eminence. "A bad sign—you lose clarity of focus. I'm the one with the Guaraní. You're the one with the competition. And nobody just 'blanks out'."

"Maybe I should stop," said Jill. "Maybe I should just shave my legs and drop out of that competition. I'm tired of being an alternative."

"Alternatives mean choices," said His Eminence. "Nothing more stressful to the human race than a real honest to goodness choice. And let's cut the crap about just wanting to be an alternative at that competition."

"Oh, please." Jill was fairly sure she did not want to hear the rest of this.

"You felt a loss of power, the result of being part of a larger group," said His Eminence. "You needed to define your-self through a manipulation of your peers. And now you have them all by the balls, if you'll pardon the expression. If you didn't, they wouldn't be treating you this way. This power grab of yours has been very successful, Jill."

"Get lost," said Jill. "Get the hell out of my head."

"You invited me in," said His Eminence. "I feel quite at home here. And you couldn't get where you wanted without me."

"We don't want the same thing," said Jill.

"Just don't go stepping in front of any more real trains, Jill," said His Eminence. "Now, would you excuse me, please? I hear the natives singing."

OVERHEAD, the library's fluorescent lighting droned on like very distant helicopters. Jill sighed. She was researching the ancient Britons for her Latin term presentation. The Sax-ons seemed about as lively as Stonehenge.

Someone slid into the seat opposite her. "Hi," said Cal. Without a chess set in front of him, he looked out of focus, hallucinatory. "You haven't been in for a game in a while."

"Yeah. I've been meeting a friend after school every day," Jill explained. "Bertram figured out how to use his knights yet?"

Cal snorted. "I could take off both rooks, go into deep sleep and beat him. What're you working on?"

In Jill's brain, something clicked. "I'm researching a kind of . . . psychology report for my social history class," she lied.

Cal glanced at the book she had open before her. "Saxons Go Psycho," he said. "Coming soon to a theater near you."

"Nah," said Jill. "That's another one I'm doing for Latin. I'm trying to find out about blanking out."

His Eminence chuckled. "Nice try, but it won't work."

"Blanking out?" Cal repeated.

"Yeah, like, if you're standing at a street corner and all of a sudden you sort of blank out and think there's no traffic or something and you step out. You think that's possible?"

Cal shrugged. "Sure. Happens to people all the time. Most of them end up dead, so it's kind of hard to do research on them."

"Well, why d' you think it happens?" Jill persisted.

Cal shrugged again. "Death wish. Suicidal. Y' know, not enough guts to do it yourself, so you just pretend there's no traffic and step out. *Splat!* Instant recycling." He looked at her calmly.

"Oh," Jill managed.

"That your next survey topic?" he asked.

"No. The *Telegraph* fired me."

"Congratulations." Cal proffered his hand. "They only weed out the intelligent ones."

"Thanks." Jill felt dazed.

Cal stood up. "Well, come in and we'll have a game soon, eh?"

"You bet," Jill said. She watched him leave.

"Told you so," His Eminence murmured. "That Cal is a very bright young man. Maybe I should switch brains."

"Anytime, Emmie," Jill sighed.

"I THINK YOU KNOW something about Liza that I don't." Dwayne leaned against Jill's bedroom doorframe in his James Dean pose.

Jill put down her health text. "Huh?" she asked.

Dwayne sat on the edge of her bed. "It's just a feeling I've got," he said. "You know something I don't."

"I don't think she meant to tell me." Jill said. "At least, not me in particular. It just came out of her one afternoon when you weren't there. I don't think she could hold it in."

"Well, why didn't you tell me?" demanded Dwayne.

"She didn't tell you. She told me," frowned Jill.

"Yeah, but . . . " Dwayne's gaze drifted across her walls, then shifted back to her. "Tell me. I want to know what it is."

Some sort of reference book I am, Jill thought. Find the

right page. Read the appropriate paragraphs. Put me back on the shelf. "Why d' you want to know?" she countered.

"What d' you mean, why do I want to know?"

"I'm sorry," said Jill quickly. "I know you care about her."

"I've never felt this way before, Jill. I just want to take care of her. Protect her, y' know? Be with her. I'd like to get her to be able to go into the cafeteria, meet my friends. Ah, they'll probably make some baby-sitting jokes. They just don't really get what's going on. But they're good guys."

It was a trick of the light. That was why the bed was lengthening, Dwayne moving farther and farther away. Jill felt herself float up until she hovered, her back against the ceiling, not really listening to him talk. His Eminence waved at her as he floated in the opposite corner. Get a grip, she thought.

"D' you think you're in love with her?"

Dwayne did not move but continued staring at a floor-board. It seemed almost as if it was he who had asked himself the question.

"Yeah," he said finally. "I think I am. It's a weird feeling, Jill. Gushy and weird."

"Are you going to start talking roses and perfume?" demanded Jill.

"D' you think she likes me?" asked Dwayne.

"Yes," said Jill. "But I wouldn't try kissing her or anything. Not yet."

"No, no," said Dwayne hastily.

"And I would stop carrying condoms in your pocket," Jill added. "What if she ever put her hand in there?"

"How'd your hand get in there?" demanded Dwayne.

Jill ducked the question, fast.

"Okay, I'll tell you what she told me," she said.

His Eminence chuckled.

"It's kind of heavy duty, though," she added.

"Can't get much worse," said Dwayne.

"Yes, it can," said Jill, grimly.

This was weird inside, she thought. She knew this would shake Dwayne up pretty bad. She didn't want to hurt him, and yet, she did—part of her did. How could she love him and want to hurt him at the same time? It was like being two different people. If she could somehow tell Dwayne about it without hurting him, then maybe she could ignore this feeling of wanting to hurt him. But how? It was like trying to walk in the snow without leaving footprints.

"It was her older brother," she said.

Jill watched what the words did, the eyes turning suddenly for her face, the quickening breath. Dwayne blinked.

"Jill?" His voice sounded thin, rising.

"What?" She pushed past His Eminence, trying to reach Dwayne. She grasped his shoulder, swung her other arm around him and hung onto him. Her big solid brother. He gripped her arms as she hugged him from behind, gripped her arms so tight they began to throb. The pain blocked out His Eminence. Jill concentrated on the hurt, kept it close, real.

They stayed this way for a long time.

DOWN AT THE OTHER END of the hallway, a group of boys were kicking a hackey sack around. Liza was at her bi-weekly psychiatric appointment, and Dwayne was at basketball practice. Jill had executed Bertram in an after-school chess game and was headed home. As she approached, the boys began to throw the hackey sack at one another, ducking and howling. Someone missed, and the hackey sack thudded into the wall of lockers. Impressed by the echoes of the impact, Jill considered turning back but decided she was too close to the exit. One of the boys turned, bent to scoop up the hackey sack and caught her eye. It was Peter.

Oh, my god, thought Jill. They stood a moment, staring at one another. Jill started to turn around, head back down the hallway.

"Hey, Jill, catch."

He tossed the hackey sack toward her, lightly, but *en route,* it mutated to a basketball, came at her like a torpedo. With a gasp, Jill ducked. The hackey sack plopped onto the floor beside her.

"Get a grip, kiddo," said His Eminence. "This is Heart Throb, remember?"

Jill leaned against the wall, recovering from the mental basketball as Peter jogged over, leaned down and picked up the hackey sack beside her feet. He came up, close to her face, leaned on one elbow against the wall. Their position now resembled a scene out of any one of her soap opera daydreams. Jill could not meet his eyes, looked away, silent.

"I'm sorry if I scared you. I didn't mean to." His voice was friendly. She could see one of his hands fidget with the hackey sack.

"That's okay." She managed to haul her eyes over to one shoulder of his green rugby shirt. "I'm not very coordinated."

"You still taking surveys?"

"Hey, Peter, you gonna take all day?" called a voice.

Jill chanced a look at Peter's face as he turned momentarily and grinned at the speaker. "What's your rush, Coots? *Star Trek* doesn't start for another hour."

"Yeah, yeah," said the voice.

Peter turned back, his eyes catching Jill's. This close, she saw they were hazel with little flecks of green in them—something she hadn't noticed before. His entire face was a quiet apology, an unspoken reference to Arlene and the death squad. Slowly, Jill fought her way up through the flock of Monarch butterflies migrating through her stomach. She smiled at him.

"Nah. The *Telegraph* fired me. Too subversive," she said.

"They're probably right," he grinned.

"I guess."

A boy appeared at Peter's elbow. "Look, Pete, if you're gonna work on your love life, can we have the hackey sack?"

Scarlet seeped up Peter's neck and face until he looked like something out of a Persian carpet. As he turned and tossed the hackey sack at the group, Jill wanted to dissolve. "Fetch," he said. When Peter turned back, his eyes flicked uneasily across her face.

"That's okay. I've got to go anyway," she said quickly.

"Yeah. Sorry about that. Coots has a verbal problem." He turned to rejoin the group. "See you in science."

"Yeah." Jill floated past the group, turning her head so no one could see the grin that was sized for a face three times larger than hers. Peter had just talked to her. Life was so wonderful. So were his lips. Notice those lips?

"DON'T WORRY about those penises, Jill," said His Eminence. "They're only metaphors."

"You are eating my brain," complained Jill. She was in the middle of a social history class. She hoped Dwayne and Liza were taking thorough notes. Ms. Thiessen had insinuated this topic would dominate the next test, and the legate was using his argumentative tone of voice. It was loud and tended to go on and on.

"I'm a metaphor," said His Eminence. He began to chant, "I'm a metaphor, you're a metaphor, I'm a metaphor, you're a metaphor."

Jill tried to turn down the volume on His Eminence, hoping no one else would hear. "No," she replied. "I'm a human being. You're my imagination. And you're screwing up my mind."

"Ah!" observed His Eminence. "You're alive and I'm not?"

"Exactly," said Jill.

"Life is a metaphor for reality," stated His Eminence. Tipping up his wig, he very carefully began to clean the wax out of one ear with his pinkie.

"Life is a metaphor for reality?" repeated Jill. "Get real, Emmie. Life *is* reality."

"Life is a subplot in the quantum leap to reality," explained His Eminence. "You and I are flip sides of the same intent."

"Oh, no, flip sides again," groaned Jill. "You and I have nothing to do with each other, except you took a wrong turn somewhere and ended up in my head, messing up my life.

You committed genocide. I entered a competition. You are Bad. I am Good."

"But y' see, Bad and Good are also metaphors," observed His Eminence complacently. He moved on to the other ear.

"No," said Jill. "You murdered people. That is Bad. Horrible. Evil. And that's reality."

"My action was a metaphor," said His Eminence. "That makes it art, part of a reality you don't fully understand as the minor metaphor that you are."

"I think you're pretty screwed up," said Jill. "You're way out in left field as far as this world goes. You wouldn't make it through the first grade in math. What's two plus two?"

"Math," observed His Eminence, "was half a sentence in a bracket on the seven-hundred ninety-seven-thousandth page of the first draft of the Reality Thesis. It got cut from the second draft. Only human beings would've attempted to drag it back in and stick it on the first page."

"I have to pass math to graduate," complained Jill.

"Graduation is a metaphor," said His Eminence.

JILL STOOD at the podium in front of her Latin class. She was in the middle of her term presentation about the Roman invasion of Britain. She hated presentations. They required a full frontal view of mass student boredom and adaptation to systematization. It was the last class of the day. The kids sat slumped in their seats, pushing pens about their desktops. Some took notes. Mr. Sinclair sat in the back right corner, posturing interest.

Greg dropped his pencil, stooped to pick it up.

Something inside Jill, below her droning voice, focused on the pencil. The dropped pencil. She kept talking, but her eyes moved to Greg as he bent down to pick it up. The heads of the other kids swung toward Greg, then back to her. Pencil retrieved, Greg leaned back in his seat, tapping the tip . . . one, two, three.

The mouths of the kids opened. There was no sound, just their lips forming the same word, over and over. Jill fought the hypnotic effect. She kept her voice going, making noises that only Mr. Sinclair heard, if him. The word. What was the word?

"Lez." Suddenly, she could hear them, their voices quiet and insistent, inside her head.

"Lez, lez, lez."

Their silent voices were louder than the one she kept marching out of her mouth. Keep it marching, she thought. Keep words going . . . out.

Greg dropped his pencil again. Like one face, all the faces in front of her slipped into the generic loose-jawed expression.

His Eminence was in the outer corner of her left eye. She could see him from the shoulders up, the size of a postage stamp, bouncing up and down. "All that power," he smiled contemplatively. "You took all their pretty average Canadian faces and simultaneously turned them into Medusa. Very good, Jill. Very good."

It was as if a wind blew up. He whisked round and round and was suddenly gone.

Her voice could not have felt heavier. It plodded on.

TRAIN

Friday, the final list of competitors was posted on the bulletin board outside the Student Council office. It was one week before the Christmas Carousel Assembly.

"I heard there's a whole bunch of new kids who entered," Dwayne said. "Let's go see who they are."

"Ah, who cares?" said Jill.

"I do," Dwayne insisted. He pulled her off the stairs and pushed her gently down the hall. "Coming, Liza?"

There was a small crowd around the bulletin board, laughter breaking out like applause. "C'mon, let's see," urged Dwayne, grabbing the girls by their elbows and pulling them into the crowd. As her brother examined the board, Jill stared down at her feet. Beside her, Liza began to chuckle. At this, Jill figured the list might be more interesting than floor tiles. She looked up. It was on pink paper, of course.

Arlene. Karen. Cindy. Susan. Laura. Marilyn. John? Richard? Joe? Larry—

"What the hell is this?" demanded Jill.

"The football team," said Dwayne.

Jill stared at him.

"Now you've got some real competition," grinned her brother.

"What?"

Dwayne grabbed her by both arms and butted her in the stomach with his head until he had pushed her backwards out of the crowd. She collapsed against the wall, giggling. Delight put its fine touch to the edge of everything. "I love it!" said Jill. "How'd you get them to do it?"

"They thought it'd be a good joke," shrugged Dwayne. "They're okay guys, Jill." He studied her face, suddenly looked away. "Some of them thought it'd get them a few dates. One of them's interested in you."

"Oh, please," said Jill.

"Plays chess," protested Dwayne, hands raised. "I gotta go—basketball. See ya, Sis."

Jill twiddled her thumbs while Dwayne and Liza said good-bye. They were turning farewells into an art form. Finally, Dwayne sauntered down the hall.

"Oh, you're ready!" said Jill.

Liza flushed.

"C'mon." The two girls pushed open the heavy wooden doors at the school's front entrance. There was a rush from behind, the sounds of feet and voices. Then something pushed hard against the small of Jill's back. She grabbed for the railing at the top of the outside step. There was a second shove. Her feet slipped, then found their footing in the air above the icy stairs. The railing slid out of her hands.

Jill tried to circle her head with her arms. Sky met ground, the world rolling round and round. Step after step wedged concrete into her body. One leg was pulled under her, farther and farther, exploded. Jill screamed, felt the world roll over once more and settle beneath her back.

There was the sky. It had wings and circled the school building. A leg was broken beneath her, but she couldn't figure out which one. Someone was trying to help her sit up. Jill screamed again. The hands retreated from her shoulders.

Liza took her hand, making small whining noises. A jacket slid under her head. Then the secretary's face showed up where the sky had been. Her nose was huge, bigger than the school.

"An ambulance is on its way."

So many legs stood around, restless feet all in runners, pushing at the snow. Voices rustled the air. Then Liza let go of her hand. Jill felt the heat leave her palm. Blurred at the edges, Liza's voice was yelling. Jill struggled to hear.

"It was you. I saw you push her. You'll pay for this, you bitch."

Jill squinted. Liza's shape loomed very dark against the sky. Jill could hardly see her head, but the hand . . . Jill saw the hand sliding under the jacket. There was something under the jacket, hidden away. No more, Jill thought. I can't take anymore. Her eyes closing, Jill screamed. She screamed and screamed and screamed.

Then a man's voice was speaking. "Calm down, here." The voice crawled into her ear, going around and around. It began to circle the inside of her skull. Jill opened her eyes.

"Where does it hurt?" asked the man. Another big nose.

"Where's Liza?" asked Jill.

"Here I am." Liza's face poked over the other edge of sky.

"Give it to me," Jill ordered. "I don't care what it is—you give it to me. Right now."

"I didn't do anything," said Liza. "When you started screaming . . . I didn't do anything."

"Give it to me." Jill felt herself sweat as the man, tired of waiting for an answer, began to check her leg. "I'll scream again," she warned. "Until you slide it into my pocket."

Liza stared off at a horizon.

"Five," began Jill, "four, three . . . "

Liza slid a smooth elongated object into Jill's coat pocket. "I'm coming in the ambulance," she said.

"DOES IT HURT?" ASKED LIZA WARILY.

"Yup," grunted Jill. She balanced herself on two crutches. They made the floor seem a good deal farther off. Thick lines of pain throbbed on her arms, back, bum, legs. "But not a cosmic kind of hurt. Wanna sit down?" She hobbled to a set of orange and blue chairs in the hospital waiting room.

Liza followed. "Your parents are coming. The school called them."

"Help me put my leg up," Jill ordered. Liza hauled a chair over and placed Jill's cast on it.

"Okay?"

"Yup," said Jill. She spoke slowly. "That was stupid, Liza. I mean, stupid."

Liza talked rapidly. "You've never been raped. You don't know what it's like."

"I don't mean stupid to carry it," said Jill. "I mean stupid to advertise it like that. You want it back? Here." She handed the Exacto knife back to Liza. The other girl's eyes narrowed.

"Why're you giving it back?" she asked. "I thought you took it to make some kind of point."

"I was scared you were going to use it," said Jill. "You're not still planning to, are you?"

"No," said Liza. She grinned. "No."

"Well, then, take it. If it makes you feel safer, good." Jill added reflectively, "Maybe I should get one." They both stared at the small smooth-handled knife in Liza's thin hand. "We weren't enough protection?"

The dark eyes glanced quickly away. "You couldn't be," Liza said softly. "It's in my head, y' know? You can't get there."

"No," said Jill. "I guess not."

Liza put the knife in her jacket pocket. "It does make me feel safer. It's pretty small, but I heard of a case where this woman stabbed the guy in the leg with it. She got away." She sat silently, then said, "I'm sorry. I didn't mean to get mad at you. I'm a jerk. You break your leg, and I get mad at you."

"Mad at me?"

"When I said that you didn't know what it was like to get raped. I'm sorry."

Jill stared at her. "Two hours ago, you were willing to commit murder for me. Get mad at me anytime you want. I know you're a better friend than anyone else in that damn school. Most of them won't even talk to me these days. Just get unmad after the mad part, okay?"

Liza's eyes were getting teary. Jill felt a huge need to keep all conversation very calm, far away from emotions. His Eminence nodded thoughtfully. "That would be wise, Jill," he said. "Yes, I think so."

"Now that I think about it," Jill added dryly, "a little murder would've done Karen good. Y' know, a few stabs to the heart, maybe a few deeper ones in the stomach. Then a neck slash. It was Karen, wasn't it? I saw her in that group around the bulletin board."

"I don't know her," said Liza. "I'm just glad you didn't hit your head. You went over and over."

"Funny thing," said Jill. The event stretched out, repeating itself in her head. "Funny, wasn't it? So many people on those steps. That sudden big rush. I should've seen people spread out in front of us. But no one was there. They were all behind us. Funny thing, eh?"

"Nobody even bumped me," muttered Liza. "She pushed you."

"Too far maybe," mused Jill.

DECEMBER HAD MOVED inside her skin, landscaping her interior in grey snow. Colors went underground to wait for the thaw. Inside, Jill turned herself into an unmoving sunless place. No feminist mother, no Shake 'n Bake father, no repentant brother, no rape victim, no blond ponytailed bitch could get at her there. She was tired of trying to understand, trying to communicate. It was better to shut them all out for a little while. They could come back later when she had rested up. For now it was just Jill and His Eminence, floating around on his back, blowing soap bubbles out of a plastic stick with a hole in it.

Of course, her mother and father wandered around, still in that calm grey-eyed dimension, just on the other side of several generations. "How are you?" they asked. "Want another cup of cocoa? Why do you run down ice-covered steps, dear?"

"Want to autograph my cast?" Jill asked. She figured that a long list of names belonged there, starting with Dwayne's and Liza's.

"Very astute of you," commented His Eminence.

Dwayne and Liza seemed to want to play Spite and Malice with her all Saturday afternoon. No one wanted to acknowledge the purplish bruises darkening on Jill's arms. Even in the soft armchair, it was hard to find a position that compromised with the welts across her bum and legs. Meaningful conversation occurred between the comings and goings of parents. "Liza says someone pushed you," said Dwayne. "I heard a rumor about that."

"It felt like a pretty motivated push," said Jill. "But I didn't see anything."

"What'd she look like?" asked Dwayne.

He doesn't want to believe this, Jill thought.

"She's blond, tall. She was wearing a school jacket," said Liza.

"D' you have last year's yearbook?" asked Jill. She flipped through Dwayne's book and found Karen's picture. "Is this her?"

"Yup," said Liza.

"What the hell would Karen Ezacko push you down the stairs for?" demanded Dwayne. "How d' you know her?"

"She's in my year," said Jill. "We're in the same gym class."

"That doesn't mean she wants to break your leg," said Dwayne.

She felt very tired, like a car windshield in the rain with the wipers malfunctioning. His Eminence was dimly outlined in light, carefully considering this conversation. "You don't want to share this power, Jill," he warned. "If you tell them, they'll take over and change things."

Jill reached over and touched Dwayne's arm. Yes, it was real. "What's the matter?" he asked, surprised.

"Nothing," she said. "Karen wants me out of the competition because I stopped shaving my legs."

"Well, so what?" Dwayne looked confused, almost angry.

"It's different," said Jill. "That's enough."

"I saw her push you," said Liza. Jill felt the warmth of her support. "She did it on purpose."

"Haven't you heard the rumor she started about me being a lesbian?" asked Jill.

"Yeah." Dwayne flopped back on the sofa. "I told them to shut up, or I'd beat the shit out of them."

"What if I were?" asked Jill. "What would you do then?"

"Very good penny there, Jill," said His Eminence. "You just derailed another relationship."

Dwayne lay back on the sofa, staring at the ceiling. Suddenly, he flung his handful of cards away. "Are you?" he demanded without looking at her.

Liza folded herself into obscurity.

"No," said Jill. "I don't think so."

Dwayne continued to examine the ceiling. "I don't like it when you play mind games, Jill."

"Just so long as I am who you want me to be?" Jill asked softly.

Dwayne was jerked upright, face rigid. "Is that what you think?"

I'm tired, Jill thought. Dwayne's face hung there, staring into her eyes like some wall-sized painting.

"Look how you can twist him around," approved His Eminence, settling back in an armchair.

"No," said Jill. "But what if I told you, 'Yes, I'm a lesbian'? Things would be different then?"

"Of course they'd be different," said Dwayne. "You'd be different."

Liza started picking up the scattered cards.

"D' you want to charge her?" asked Dwayne. "Call the cops?"

Stillness at the center. To keep that stillness, that calm— that was all Jill wanted. Grey sky, grey earth. No movement, no thought. Just a little quiet on the tracks between trains.

"Let's play again," she said.

TRAIN

That evening, Dwayne and Liza went to a movie. They asked her to go along, but Jill refused, saying she would watch a movie on the VCR with Mom and Dad. Dwayne did not notice her deserted mood. "Have a good time," she said.

JILL LISTENED to *The Mission* soundtrack. The music circled the room, bending back in on itself. She had known it would do this to her—demand the quiet, the greyness inside go away, make all her emotions come back. The voices started, small sudden embers, down in her gut. They grew. There was no keeping them back, all that sound and beauty inside. With it came the pain. Why did she have to be so different? Why did she have to think about everything? But it was so exciting to think. It made her feel alive. Why was everyone else so afraid of their brains?

His Eminence blossomed in her head. "You're mixing your metaphors again, Jill," he warned. "Save your own skin. You need to keep your outlines very carefully fixed."

His voice was washed away in the river of singing. The voices wrapped Jill round and round with movement. There was no stillness anywhere. Everywhere inside, she was moving. She had lost her center. Her edges, her outline, began to float away.

Screams of joy. The Guaraní, singing as the soldiers shot them, screamed with a joy that was sent out from their mouths to pass from living ear to ear, round an earth of ears. As long as an ear lived, the scream would go on, exquisite as art. Their murder had become art, just as His Eminence had said it would.

Jill turned her back on His Eminence. She heard him laugh softly. "No, Jill," he said. "You cannot banish me. Not from truth. Truth is the greatest art, and that is where I live."

That was where the tears came from, the knowledge that somehow she, Jill, had turned a story about a terrible murder into a song that inspired her, kept her going—kept her from shaving her legs. It's sick, she thought. Really sick. He's right. His Eminence doesn't lie.

147

IT WAS THE LAST MONDAY before the competition. The week swung like a sandbag between Jill's crutches, from agony to exhaustion, and back again. Her bruises had darkened to an ominous purple-black. Dwayne and Liza escorted Jill everywhere, fencing her in with determined conversation. Liza's hand continually hovered about her right pocket.

Dwayne did not seem to be really there in his conversation, though he showed up for sentence fragments. He could not figure out why this had happened to her. Jill watched anger grow in her brother, watched the sense of betrayal that formed his expression, the line about his mouth. This was new to him, Jill realized, wondering briefly if he would like to meet His Eminence. Probably beat the legate up, though. Wouldn't like the wig. Or the attitude.

It had taken Jill twenty-four hours to realize the major benefit of broken limbs. She was now exempt from gym class. Still, her awkward approach stopped hallways of conversation, turned kids' faces to backs. Even the teachers seemed to have eyes behind their eyes, one set for seeing the class as a whole and one pair just for her. Had they all heard the rumors? No one had charged Karen, she knew that.

Inside her head, His Eminence sat and watched. He was waiting for the finale.

THE THREE OF THEM sat in a back corner of the cafeteria, Jill on the outside, her cast stretched out along the aisle. With Dwayne opposite her, no one considered calling her a "lez," but Jill could feel minds around her thinking it. *Paranoia,* she thought. Theirs or yours?

Fewer guys stopped and joked with her brother these days. Dwayne never mentioned it, but Jill could see the guarded look in his eyes as more and more kids simply walked by. He just gets quieter and quieter, Jill thought. Well, most of the time. Right now, he was teaching Liza how to arm wrestle while eating an ice cream cone.

"Jill." It was Cal. He stood beside her, his gaze flicking toward Dwayne.

"Hi. Sit down." Jill grinned a little. She had never thought anyone could influence Calvin Harding's nerves, but then she had never looked at her football captain brother from Monster Brain's eyes. Dwayne was very involved with feeding Liza ice cream. Neither noticed Cal.

He sat down gingerly, leaving as much space as possible between him and Dwayne's rugby shirt. "Your leg is the topic of the hour."

"Yeah? What are the masses saying?" She offered him some of her french fries.

"No way. Boiled alive in cholesterol." Cal opened a bag of dried fruit and nuts. "The proletariat is muttering away about the competition. Well, and about your mushed up leg."

"Yeah, I can feel the vibes," Jill muttered.

"Gonna go through with it?"

Jill's stomach clenched. Cal's look was very direct. Everyone else had assumed she would continue onward, unswerving. Dwayne and Liza, her parents—they had all been very encouraging.

"I dunno. Haven't thought about it."

His Eminence glared at Cal as he chewed thoughtfully on an apricot. "You don't have to. You can back out. I mean, Karen and her loser friends are just a bunch of tapeworms, but . . ."

"Yeah, I know," said Jill. "Corporate executive tapeworms."

Cal grinned. "Yeah. Well, I gotta go. I left Bertram trying to figure out how to escape a check. There is a way—"

"But you have to know how to use a knight, right?" Jill finished.

"You got it." Cal paused. "Break a leg, eh?"

His Eminence stared after Cal disapprovingly. Beside her, Dwayne and Liza finished off the ice cream. Somewhere, Jill felt a weight lift slightly. I do have a choice, she thought.

His Eminence sighed. "After your brother rearranged the entire event for you?"

Dwayne, wiping ice cream off his face, winked at her. Jill regarded the congealed gravy sprawled across a french fry thoughtfully. "It's just that I hadn't thought of it lately as a choice, Emmie, m' dear," she said to the legate. "Puts an entirely different slant on it, don't you think?"

WEDNESDAY, they were sitting on the stairwell, eating lunch when Liza reached down to scratch her ankle and her sleeve pulled up.

"What's on your arm?" Dwayne said.

Liza pulled back against the wall. She stared at them silently. She was wearing the dark blue sweatshirt. The sleeve rested halfway up one forearm. Long dark scabs twisted on her skin. Liza blinked a few times. Jill watched her eyes grow more and more empty, as if something was receding, going away from them. She's looking for that grey place inside, Jill thought. No emotions. No pain.

"Why did you do this?" Dwayne asked. His voice was hoarse, low.

Liza just stared. She must've done it with her fingernails, Jill thought. Please, God, not the Exacto knife.

Somewhere in her head, someone flicked the On switch. She began to hear the Guaraní sing. I do it, too, Jill thought. I do this to myself.

"Liza," said Jill, "next time, scratch me?"

Nobody looked at anybody else.

Jill continued. "And I'll scratch Dwayne, and Dwayne'll go play football."

There was only the sound of their breathing. Jill reached over and ran a fingertip gently along the surface of one of the scabs. It felt rough and strong.

"Okay," said Liza softly.

Slowly, Dwayne reached one arm up and around Liza and pulled her toward him. As his arms went around the thin shoulders, Jill tensed, waiting for Liza's sudden explosion into fear. It did not happen. Dwayne sat, eyes closed, one cheek resting on top of Liza's head, and Liza, off balance on her stair, curled into him, face hidden beneath her dark hair. Looking at them, Jill felt some of the darkness lift, up and away.

"Um, Dwayne," said Liza, after a moment.

"Yeah?" asked Dwayne, eyes still closed.

"This is the very best hug I've ever had, but my bum's getting sore."

They started to laugh, all of them. It was the same laugh, shared by three bodies, and it went on and on.

"See if I ever hug you again," Dwayne said. "No appreciation." He held Liza's forearm gently in both hands and looked up at her face. "I don't understand this. I want to, but I don't."

"I'm glad you don't," Liza said, looking down at him. "If you did, I'd be worried for you." For a long moment, they looked at each other in silence. "I won't do it again, Dwayne. Okay?"

Dwayne hesitated, frowned slightly. "Okay."

SCIENCE CLASS ON CRUTCHES was an ominous prospect. Jill hesitated outside the door and listened to the hubbub of voices inside. A few of her classmates passed her without comment. How could she go in there, she wondered, and ignore Arlene's bulldog sneers? If she waited too long though, the bell would go and she would have to thump her way to her desk as the rest of the class watched, secure on their stools. Shifting the weight of her books between hand and crutch grip, Jill heaved herself up and swung through the door.

As usual, the boys decorated Arlene's half of the desk, blocking the aisle. "Excuse me," Jill said to a bum whose torso leaned, oblivious, across the desk.

Around her, loud conversation continued. "Excuse me," Jill repeated. The boy's face turned slightly toward her, then away. It was Lyle.

"Careful," murmured His Eminence.

No one moved. Normally, Jill would have squeezed by, but with crutches, she had become the size of an apartment block and the option was no longer available. She poked a crutch at Lyle's shoe. He did not budge.

Jill knew he felt the tip of her crutch against his foot. She saw Arlene's grinning eyes flick over her. Suddenly, fatigue and pain swirled out from Jill's legs and armpits. She was going to have to stand there until the bell rang and the boys decided it was time to go to their seats.

Jill fought a desire to faint, disappear from the scene in any convenient manner. Her books slid out of her grip. Turning her head, Jill saw Peter, her books now in his hand, lean over so that his mouth was next to Lyle's ear.

"Lay off." Peter's voice was harsh. "Just lay off with the bully stuff, y' hear me?"

Lyle froze into position. Slowly, all conversation at Arlene's desk, then out across the classroom, subsided. In perfect silence, Lyle stood up and brushed by Peter. The aisle gaped wide open ahead of Jill. She hobbled around to her side of the desk and sat down, placing the crutches beside the desk. It was hard to decide whether to look at Peter or not. He had probably just destroyed all social possibilities in his life by helping her out. She did not want to make it worse.

"Are you okay? It's hard to sit on a stool like that. I know; I broke my leg in grade seven." He set her books down, his voice quiet, determined. Around them, voices began again.

"Thanks," Jill whispered soundlessly. Her eyes, like two anchors, were pulling her downward.

There was a pause. Then Peter's face, still flushed, appeared opposite her, chin on the desktop. "One point seven," he said.

Laughter spurted out of her, and she found her voice, looked at him. "Thanks."

His face sobered. "My privilege," he said.

The bell rang.

LIZA WAS CUTTING Jill's black sweats to shorts. Jill hung onto the washroom counter. Neither spoke as the metal slid in a circle around Jill's legs, making the cool scissoring noise.

The waiting period fell away, exposed a black welt across Jill's calf. In the mirror, she could see the long bruises that still lay in startling relief across both arms.

So this was it. On the stage, the Christmas Carousel assembly was about to begin. Now that she was here, Jill was not sure she remembered why she had wanted to enter in the first place. The action itself seemed silly, without meaning. Walking across a stage in a cast and an unshaved leg—what was the point?

His Eminence had temporarily vacated her head. For the first time in weeks, her mind was her own. Jill knew Liza could feel her shaking. "Liza, come up on stage with me?"

Liza's mouth tightened. She stooped and began to pick up pieces of black material from the floor.

"Be my crutch?"

Liza placed the cloth on the counter, then stood very still, looking down.

"Please? I can't do this by myself."

Liza glanced at her. Jill hung onto the other girl's dark eyes with her own. It was very quiet. They were both remembering their afternoon, months ago, in the rain—the way it had changed things, made things possible. Again, Jill touched the sleeve over the scabs on Liza's forearm.

"Please? Help me?"

The scissors Liza held clattered as she set them down on the counter. "I'd like to shoot my brother," Liza said. "I'd like to shoot the bugger all over the place." There was a pause. Unsmiling, Liza looked at Jill. "Let's go."

Competitors were supposed to meet backstage. Jill hobbled in, leaning on Liza. Immediately, the football team gathered around them, grinning, their gaze skittering over her bruises. They all wore gym shorts. Some were bare chested. Jill tightened her grip on Liza's wrist. Bare chests made her nervous.

But Liza was laughing into her ear. "Jill, look at their legs."

They had shaved.

MISSION IMPOSSIBLE

Every member of the football team sported an ankle-to-hem hairless surface. The boys were entirely pleased with themselves, sporting a team grin. "Hell, I cut myself up all over the place," complained one.

"I got my sister to do it," said another.

"What d' you do with them ankle bones?" demanded a third.

A grin waylaid Jill's face. Then she saw Peter, standing to one side. His legs, too, were clean shaven. He looked at her and shrugged.

"I always shave my legs for swim meets. Thought I might as well enter." He grinned.

Those lips, she thought.

"You've got an unfair advantage," Peter said. "Know who the judges are?"

"No."

"Well, your brother, for one. And Rob Warner." Peter made a significant pause. "And Karen Ezacko."

Karen. Jill's grin shrunk to a very fine line.

"Dwayne got her to withdraw from the competition and become a judge," Liza explained.

"So, how does that give me an advantage?" Jill asked.

"Rob Warner flunked a French test because he kept conjugating your name," someone else said.

"Oh, please," protested Jill.

"Plays chess," commented another.

"Plus, you're last in line," said another. "That gives you the best chance. Out of sight, out of mind—you know the mentality. If I don't place here, I won't be able to enter the Miss World Pageant." He walked off, moaning, "We ain't got a chance at our biggest dream, guys."

Jill and Liza stood at the end of the line, watching each competitor walk out. Some of the girls laughed, but it was a tight sound. A few looked openly angry. This was not the way it had been planned. Beyond the curtain, the large crowd whistled and made catcalls as the girls walked out. There were waves of laughter at the boys. Finally, it was Jill's turn.

They started off. Jill sweated. Beside her, she heard Liza's heavy breathing. They passed the curtain. She could not see much in the bright footlights. There was Dwayne, with Rob and Karen, behind a podium on the opposite side of the stage.

"We have to walk around," Jill hissed at Liza.

"Which way?" Liza whispered. They pulled in opposite directions. There was laughter from the crowd. The two girls reconnected. Between the thumps of her cast, the crowd was settling down, becoming uneasily quiet. The bruises were making their impact. Jill tried to posture her good leg this way and that, was rewarded with trickles of laughter, a few whistles.

There was the feeling of an immense lack, as if she was at the center of nothing real. Jill felt no connection to anyone. It was if they were all just another part of the emptiness. Something important was missing. What was it? Everyone was here—Liza, Dwayne, the football team. She was here. The stars of the show, her leg hairs, were giving a classic performance.

The two girls jerked their way off the stage. "Oh, god, it's over," said Jill. A long sigh shuddered through her body. "I'm so glad this is over." She slumped onto a chair.

"Listen," said Liza. On this side of the curtain, the stage speech was muffled. "I'm going closer to hear."

Jill watched Liza join the crowd of competitors at the curtain. There was a roar, then giant laughter. The audience clapped. A boy at the stairs jumped up, fists in the air and ran onto the stage.

There goes first place, Jill thought wearily.

The audience began to clap in rhythm. Jill closed her eyes, trying to keep the beat out of her head. It was dark and empty in there. Empty . . . that was it. His Eminence was gone. He had not had the decency to stick around and see her triumph, her penny on the track, her cross over the waterfall or whatever the hell this was supposed to be.

The applause died. There was Dwayne's voice again. More

laughter. He could still hold a crowd in the palm of his hand. Nothing had changed. Well, yes—they got along now. Jill opened her eyes and saw Liza whirl, then come running toward her.

"You're second," she grinned. "They said they couldn't give you first because you only had one leg."

Jill felt her heart begin to kick at her chest. She wanted to smile. She was sure she wanted to smile. The football team began pulling at her arms. Liza slid under one shoulder. The brief shadow of the curtain zoomed by and she was in the middle of the bright lights again. There was Dwayne's voice over the microphone. "And now, second prize . . . "

Jill blinked, trying to see. She saw the stage with Dwayne coming toward her. Then she blinked. Black, empty, no one there. The stage showed up again, Dwayne closer. His face poked into her own, triumphant, as he placed two hands around her head. Everything went black. No one. She felt Dwayne's big sloppy kiss on her forehead.

The audience was clapping again now, more certain of her as runner-up. In rhythm, they clapped and pounded their feet until it echoed off the walls, catching her heart, forcing it into their pulse. Her entire body seemed to vibrate with each pound.

Dwayne reached behind himself and unhooked something from the back of his jeans. Bringing it around, he shook it in the air. A pair of nylons dangled in front of her.

"Your prize," he bawled into her ear and shoved it into her hand. Then he turned to the audience and unhooked something else from his back pocket. It was a small orange razor, the cap over the sharp edge. "Finders, keepers!" he yelled and whipped it up into the air.

Jill quickly lost sight of its orange arc. It faded somewhere beyond the footlights, beyond the beginnings of faces that blurred to blackness. Dwayne grabbed her right hand and pulled it high above her head. Still in her grip, the nylons dangled, brushing against her face. Jill swayed, tried to steady herself with her good foot. On the other side, she felt Liza take her other hand and lift it uncertainly. The rhythm of the crowd took hold of Dwayne's fist. He began to pound the air.

Jill was confused. Something—everything had gone very wrong. Dwayne held her right hand so tightly that it was difficult, with the cast, to move. On the other side, she felt Liza step back, her fingers sliding away. Liza was afraid of this crowd, its colossal mood. It was too big. Jill grabbed the girl's wrist and pulled her in behind her back. Under her fingers, she felt the scabs, large and crusty.

The beat slammed against them. Jill's head hurt. It was Dwayne winning this competition, she thought. Not her. The crowd cheered her because they thought she was part of Dwayne's joke, just like the football team. The benefits and the penalties. She could just stand there, keep her mouth shut, and she would turn into some sort of offbeat heroine, maybe make a yearbook photo as runner-up. But that was not good enough. No one knew why she was here. And she was losing her hold on Liza's arm. Jill could feel the girl slipping away. On the other side of her, Dwayne's grip tightened.

"Let her go."

Finally, he was there. The Guaraní burst into song, and His Eminence showed up in full glory, sky-size, crowding everyone else out. "Let her go," he repeated. "She's just a metaphor."

"What?" Jill stared at him. His Eminence began to bop about slightly to the beat of the crowd. "What're you talking about?" Jill asked.

"Liza," he said. "You always gotta sacrifice something for success. You got it wrong, Jill. Dwayne isn't in charge of this. You are. You're running this entire show. They changed it all for you."

"They're changing me for them," said Jill.

The memory of the train coming at her down the track was suddenly there. She was standing in for the penny on the track, the cold clinging to her face, the sound of the train rushing at her, looming large, the vibrations shaking her skin and bones like the pulse of the crowd in the auditorium.

They'll run me down, she thought. And I don't want to die in front of some train. I never wanted to go down any waterfall. This isn't about trains and waterfalls. It's about assumptions—that's what it's about.

"That's what you're about." She yelled it at His Eminence. "Assumptions. You're made up of assumptions."

Her yell broke through his hovering face, scattering it to fragments that drifted slowly away. "You're all about assumptions that things never change. That no matter what I do, nothing will or can change. You want me to think those Guaraní would've died anyway, sooner or later, but that isn't true. You made it happen because you were afraid of losing your job in Europe or getting demoted. You're just a lousy coward."

Like dirt on a rainy windowpane, His Eminence's face floated away.

With everything she had, Jill twisted out of Dwayne's grip and turned toward the back of the stage. She saw Liza, her hunched shoulders, slip behind the curtain. Jill's pulling away from Dwayne must have finally made him notice that Liza was going. When Jill turned back to face him, he had stopped waving his fist and was staring after Liza.

"Let me say something," Jill yelled into his ear. "Let me talk. Please."

For a moment, he hesitated. Please, she thought. Trust me. Can't you feel her slipping away? Slipping away, maybe for good?

Dwayne nodded and went over to the podium. As he waved his hands, the crowd settled. Their silence seemed louder than the chanting had been. Jill hobbled over to the mike. She had to hang onto the podium to stand up.

"I am afraid of you." She had not known she would say this. "I am afraid of you in large groups. Because then you make me change. You make me someone I don't want to be."

There was such a loud silence out there. It was yelling at her ears, telling her to shut up. Jill glanced away and saw Liza standing by the curtain.

Jill swallowed hard as she continued. "Why is it when there are so many people around, you feel so alone? I don't want this to be lonely. I mean, what's life all about if you're lonely? You want to trust the people around you."

The words came more quickly now. "I guess everyone knows by now I stopped shaving my legs. I just did it because I wondered why we did that. Does anyone know why? I mean, why is it important?"

No one answered.

"It must be important," Jill continued. "Everyone noticed. Pretty crazy, eh? All this trouble just because of a little difference. But I guess I found out there are people who don't care about the difference." Jill looked across the stage toward Liza. "That's all that matters, y' know—knowing you have friends."

Applause trickled out of the crowd as Jill moved away from the podium. In the back of her head, she heard the Guaraní fade out for the last time. She turned to Dwayne. "Meet us in the cafeteria for a pop?"

He stared at her, then nodded. "Yup," he said, then added, "Way to go, Sis."

Liza was waiting for her at the other end of the stage and gave her an arm to lean on. They found their way out of the bright lights. Behind the stage, Peter, the football team and the girls gave her weak smiles. No one had much to say as she and Liza passed by and out into the hallway.

No one was out there. They were halfway down the echoing hall when Liza stopped, turning to face her. Her face was pale, the dark eyes hesitant. "Did you do this for me?" she asked. "All this stuff—was it for me?"

"No," Jill said quietly.

Sudden light coming through a window lit up every angle of Liza's face. Jill smiled. Even if it was only life-sized, it was so much more beautiful than His Eminence's. No Warp, Jill pleaded silently. No Warp.

Liza grinned. "You gonna shave your legs now?"

A laugh took Jill. "Y' know, I haven't even thought about it." She shrugged. "Decisions, decisions." Leg hair, penises, the cheerleading squad—she didn't have to figure it all out *now*. Leave something to think about for ten minutes down the line.

Behind them was the sound of running feet as Dwayne caught up to them. The three of them went on together down the hall.